THE BEEKEEPER

JULIET MOORE

Created with Vellum

THE BEEKEEPER

Elizabeth felt the bee's stinger pierce the skin at the base of her neck. Its buzzing reverberated through her head as she swatted it away. The bee, like so many evacuees, must have been displaced thanks to the hurricane. But the Roosevelt Hotel was one place it clearly didn't belong, no more than Elizabeth did.

As if this two-star crap hole she called home wasn't bad enough.

She sprinted back to her room, a bottle of Diet Coke from the second floor vending machine in hand. When she heard a door open behind her, she did a quick roundabout only to see a young woman in a halter top and tiny sequined shorts slip quietly into the hallway from one of the rooms. Elizabeth sighed and turned away. Prostitutes were par for the course in this part of town, and, as long as they made it out alive, they were not really her concern. Four years as a homicide detective in Miami can give a person some interesting priorities.

The second floor hallway smelled like stale cigarettes and room service french fries. Elizabeth stepped over a spot on the carpet that looked suspiciously damp and picked up the pace again. This wasn't the kind of place she liked to wander around by herself, especially without the gun she'd gotten used to having holstered at her waist. She patted the place where her holster used to be, missing the familiar weight of it. *C'est la vie*. At least it was a suspension, not a termination, and she'd been through worse.

The hallway turned about fifty feet ahead, right about where a fluorescent ceiling fixture flickered unreassuringly. The sound of a door slamming echoed from that direction; then came the pounding of feet on vintage carpet. Elizabeth took the only option she had, which was to flatten herself against the wall and wait. A moment later, a young man came barreling around the corner.

The teenager stopped when he saw her, eyes wide, mouth slightly open, his body jerking as though he still wanted to run but couldn't get his legs to work. "It's the bees. My girlfriend is still up there. I wanted to save her, but I'm allergic. They would have killed me. Please help her!"

"More bees?" Elizabeth could still feel the painful welt on her neck. "Where is she?"

"Upstairs. At the end of the hall."

Elizabeth dropped her soda and took off in the direction the guy had come from. She reached the end of the hall, ripped open the door beneath a glowing 'EXIT' sign, and sped up a flight of stairs. The next door was heavy and stiff, scraping the floor and leaving a half-circle impression in the concrete. The hallway was dim, with only the moonlight coming through open doors.

This floor was in the midst of a renovation. The owner of the Roosevelt had initially wanted to tear it down, but was denied. So renovations began, but stopped when they became too expensive. Elizabeth rushed inside, stumbling over a metal toolbox. It clanged against her sneaker, echoing down the dark corridor. The doors to the rooms were propped open, revealing detritus-filled corners. She tried to move as fast as she could.

She hurried toward the executive suite, closing the distance in just a few strides. Then she was upon the double doors of the large, once-luxurious room. The entire floor was quiet, except for the distant hum of an air conditioner.

The doors to the suite were open; she went in. The hum she'd been hearing suddenly became much louder. And it was no air conditioner.

Bees filled the room like a storm cloud.

Elizabeth gasped and backed up, her back hitting the doorframe. The guy had said there were bees, but...

Her gaze fell upon a human-sized shape on the floor. She focused on the unmoving object until she realized she was looking at a prostrate woman—the abandoned girlfriend.

She wanted nothing to do with the bees that were hovering within the suite, blurring her vision. Unless the woman on the ground was severely allergic, she should still be alive. *To protect and serve,* Elizabeth mouthed silently.

Elizabeth felt the bugs hit her as she ran, pelting her like hail. She ran until her toes touched the legs of the comatose woman. Then she bent over quickly and gripped the woman's ankles. In the unavoidable pause, she felt the prick of a stinger on the small of her back.

The woman's ankles felt too cold, too soft. Elizabeth's gaze traveled up the woman's body, even as another bee tried to sting her wrist. She was holding onto a dead body, looking into vacant eyes set deep in a half-rotted face. She released the woman's ankles and stumbled backward.

This couldn't be the girlfriend. This wasn't a woman who'd been attacked by bees moments ago. This was a woman who was long dead.

As Elizabeth struggled to right herself, she heard a nearby moan. She looked over and saw another woman, still moving.

Elizabeth crawled over the short distance and, with a good initial pull to get the victim going, she yanked the woman, not bothering to avoid the wet cardboard boxes and old carpeting covering the floor. She dragged her over the threshold and into the hallway, then slammed the double door shut behind her with a good heel kick, hoping the bees would stay close to the hive.

They didn't, she realized, as she felt another stinger in the fleshy part of her arm.Immediately she went back to dragging. It felt like an eternity passed before she got the woman into the stairwell. She felt the woman's neck for a pulse, found one, and sighed in relief. Then she called 911. Because, whether she liked it or not, at that moment, Elizabeth was a civilian. She turned her attention back to the woman.

Her face was swollen with red bumps, making her features difficult to distinguish. One of her eyes was swollen grotesquely. Tiny slivers were poking out of the woman's skin. Stingers. Elizabeth knew that bee stingers continued to pump poison even after being detached from its victim. So she started to scratch away the stingers she could see, hoping to lessen the amount of venom entering the woman's system.

The woman woke with a start and tried to sit up, pushing against Elizabeth's chest.

"You have to move! The bees are everywhere."

Elizabeth held her down. "I got you. You're safe now."

The woman pressed her fingers against her scalp. "My head hurts. Am I going to be all right?"

"The stings aren't life threatening. Your head probably hurts from when you fell. You knocked yourself unconscious."

"I feel so weak." She closed her eyes. "Did you see the body?"

Elizabeth leaned back. "Yes."

"She didn't even look human. It was awful. Please don't let me die."

The soothing sound of professional, efficient talk floated up the stairwell when the door onto the landing beneath opened with a loud squeak. "The paramedics are here. Everything is going to be fine."

The woman's darkly shadowed eyelids fluttered and, with a burst of energy, she grabbed Elizabeth's arm and squeezed it tightly. "What about Brian? Is he still in there?"

"He's fine. He's the one who sent me."

Two paramedics appeared on the landing in a rush. One of them knelt next to the woman with a blood pressure machine and Elizabeth quickly filled him in on the situation. A few minutes later, he was lifting the woman into his arms to carry her downstairs.

Elizabeth gave her an encouraging smile as they disappeared down the stairs, then frowned and looked down at her hands just as her phone rang. "Hello?"

Captain McQuinn's voice blared through her phone. "So Stratton, am I to understand you stumbled onto a body?"

"Yes. Literally," Elizabeth replied after knocking the volume down a few notches.

"I guess you're back on duty."

"Not a moment too soon," she said, pacing in the cramped stairwell landing.

"Okay, stay right there. I'll send someone to assist. Get the investigation going."

She looked at the door, happy that it was heavy and left no gaps around the edges—that was probably due to fire codes, but it worked for bees, too. "But we have a problem."

"Already?"

"The corpse is in the middle of a room full of bees."

Clear as day, she could hear Captain McQuinn chewing his omnipresent tobacco. He spit loudly and cleared his throat. "Then I guess we're going to need a beekeeper."

Elizabeth retrieved her soda from the second floor, and then went back to the stairwell to wait it out. She really should have asked the Captain whom he was sending. Now it was all she could think about. Her partner had been transferred to Miami Beach, against his will, and that had been the end of them. Both professionally and personally.

It was just as well. Their fooling around was what had gotten them in trouble in the first place.

When she heard the door below open and shut, she stood up and peered over the railing. She didn't think it was overly paranoid, considering she was in the wrong part of town. It was also unfortunate that she would still be staying here, as living at her home was not possible due to hurricane damage. Even during normal times, Miami was a bad place to receive timely construction work. After a hurricane, when demand suddenly exceeded supply, it was an excruciating wait. And if there were another hotel that was in her price range, she'd love to hear about it.

As soon as she saw a tuft of dark hair, she knew who it was. She didn't know if she was happy or sad. One thing was for certain: the night just got more interesting. She jumped back to lean casually against the wall, as though she couldn't care less who was coming. Except that she cared greatly. Of all the people to be the first person to see after the *incident* and her three-month suspension, why did it have to be him?

She finished smoothing down her hair moments before he appeared on the landing.

Nick Fiorello was wearing a grin and a three-piece suit. "Long time no see."

"Have I missed a lot?"

"Tons. Just last week I got a haircut."

She felt her cheeks stretch into a smile then stopped herself. "Seriously."

"Seriously? Some people died. Some people lived. Luckily, I was in the latter category."

"Lucky for who?" Elizabeth let herself smile, but turned away. Facing the door, she said, "It's good to be back."

He joined her and reached for the handle. "So what have you found for me, Miss Marple?"

"Found for you?" She grabbed his wrist. "You do

realize Captain McQuinn said I could consider myself back on the job?"

Nick looked at where she touched him and raised an eyebrow. "It was just an expression. Is it gruesome in there?"

"No, it's not that," she said, gently pulling him away from the door. "Did they brief you on the bees?"

"What's a few bees?"

"It's not a few bees. It's an infestation."

"Sounds exciting." He was looking down, which made her realize she still hadn't let go of him.

Feeling her face heat up, she snatched her hand away. "The beekeeper should arrive sometime tonight. Until then, we're just going to make sure our scene isn't compromised any more than it already is."

"Giving orders already?"

"Be serious, Nick," she said. "It's strange for me, coming back under these circumstances. I still haven't gotten over what happened."

He seemed thoughtful. "If you aren't ready, just tell the captain. You can continue to see the counselor—"

"Never mind." She looked down into the dark stairwell, the floors beneath beckoning her. On one of them was her room, where she could escape him. But that wouldn't be doing her job. "So does this mean you are my new partner?"

"Me? You wish."

"Not really."

He shook his head. "It's not official just yet, but I think you'll be paired with James Faraday. He's a new transfer from the Bradenton area. He came with me tonight."

"Then where is he?"

"He's parking the car."

"And you ditched him. You really have great people skills, you know that?"

Nick checked his phone messages. "As soon as James gets up here, I'm out. I have some other things I need to attend to. You can handle this?"

"Of course. So James won't have a ride?"

"You'll have to drop him off at the station after you're done for the night." He leaned over the railing. "I think I hear him now."

There was a door slamming from below, footsteps, and then a voice with a slightly southern twang called up to them, "You up there, Fiorello?"

Nick replied, "Yeah, come on up."

Her first impression of James Faraday when his head appeared above the railing was reassuring. He was slightly older than her—probably late thirties if she had to guess. He appeared confident, but not arrogant like Nick. James's gaze quickly took in his surroundings in a way that made Elizabeth feel like she could trust him to have her back. James was wearing a dark blue nylon jacket and was covered in rain drops. "It's raining cats and dogs out there!"

"And hurricane season just started," she replied, unable to stop herself from smiling at his hyperbole. "It's nice to meet you, James. I'm Elizabeth. Are you ready to hit the ground running?"

"I sure am," he said. "That's why I moved out here. More excitement."

She nodded. "I hope you like bees."

"What's not to love?"

Nick didn't say anything while she updated James on everything that had happened so far. Nick listened to every word, probably judging her quick summary. Finally, he said, "I'll leave you to it, then."

As he left, Elizabeth tried her best not to let her opinion of him show on her face. She put on a false smile and turned to James. "So what do you think?"

"How about you wait here for the beekeeper and I'll canvas the hotel a bit—speak to some of the employees?"

"Okay." She pulled her phone out of her pocket, wondering how she could keep busy while she waited and take her mind off what was on the other side of the door. "Reconvene here in about an hour."

James descended the stairs and was gone.

Elizabeth sat on the first step and waited.

The beekeeper changed into the uniform of his trade in one of the unlit hotel rooms along the corridor leading up to the suite. He buttoned the long-sleeved white tunic over a 'Margaritaville' t-shirt and tucked the hems of his pants into a pair of canvas boots. "So you're telling me there's a dead body in there?"

"You said that wouldn't be a problem." Elizabeth watched him slip on a pair of thick gloves and then sort through a large box full of beekeeping supplies.

"Nah, not a problem for me." He stood up and handed her a veil. "She's just lying there? Not even a sheet or anything?"

"A sheet would compromise any evidence we might collect." She slipped the veil over her head and led him into the hallway. Nick had gone to notify the night manager of what was going on.

The beekeeper approached the suite's door and deposited his box against the wall beneath shards of a broken picture frame. From the depths of the box, he produced a metal, cylindrical object that looked like a miniature Doctor Who Dalek. He opened the object, stuffed it full of crumpled newspaper and ratty twine, then lit it with a cheap gas station lighter.

She watched him pump the bellows until it produced a thick cloud of white smoke. Elizabeth coughed behind her hand, then slowly opened the door to the suite. She tried not to be obvious when she backed up quickly to let him lead the way. The fact that she was even there was progress. "Does that kill them?"

"This is just a smoker." He bent to retrieve a larger box attached to what looked like a vacuum. "If all goes according to plan, the smoke will calm them so I can suck them up. I'll relocate them to one of my apiaries."

He walked into the room with the smoker, moving very slowly and deliberately, letting the smoke collect around him like a shield. He pumped the bellows slowly as he walked, allowing long plumes of smoke to escape with each compression.

Elizabeth walked a straight line through the burgeoning cloud until she hit the opposite wall. It was dark, but there was enough ambient light to see things up close, even though the windows were blocked by heavy curtains. She pulled the curtains apart carefully, not knowing much about the habits of bees, but thinking that old curtains might be a favored hiding place. The fabric felt dusty beneath her fingertips, like it had been covered with a fine sifting of flour. This made her cough more than the smoke, but she persisted and eventually exposed the dirty window and the muted city lights the drapes had been concealing.

"The killer really did a number on her, didn't he?" The apiarist was standing at the victim's feet, staring down at what the moonlight revealed.

Elizabeth's back stiffened. "Do you mind?"

"Can't blame a guy for being curious." The smoke whirled around him in a concealing halo, tendrils of it reaching out to the dead woman on the floor.

Elizabeth crossed the room. "I need you to do your work as far away from her as possible. Understand?"

He stepped away slowly, but he was still too close to the body. When he took a second step with his boot-clad foot, there was an audible *crunch*. He froze, his other foot suspended in mid-air.

"Move."

The apiarist turned away with a pained expression. He walked to the gigantic hive, where he began working the pump and the vacuum simultaneously.

Elizabeth, biting down hard on the inside of her lip, aimed her flashlight at the floor beside the victim. The light glinted off a small pile of crushed glass. Glass that had clearly been whole moments before.

Leaving the glass for CSU to collect—and praying something crucial hadn't just been destroyed—she turned to check on the apiarist. He was working silently in the corner, barely visible amidst the swarm surrounding him.

She pulled back the curtains on another window to brighten the room even more. The room was getting alarmingly cloudy. If the smoke detectors on this level were operational, this could turn into a major disaster. So she opened both windows, paint flaking off the frames and falling around her feet like snow. Turning away, she started a preliminary sketch of the room. She found more glass under the windows and checked each pane for breakage. "I'm going to have to ask you to step very carefully. Always look before you step. Everything in this room is evidence."

"Sure thing," he replied without turning his head.

Elizabeth went back to the victim before taking another look at the room. The beam of her flashlight reflected off a thick piece of glass in the victim's hair and startled a bee that had been resting there as well. Whatever had shattered in the room had done so after the victim was already dead. That was important information.

The woman's eyes were bulging out of their red-rimmed sockets. The soft tissue on much of her face had been eaten away, leaving behind the smooth bones of her jaw and starkly exposed teeth. As Elizabeth leaned in a little closer, a fat ant crawled out of one of the dark crevices. Shuddering, she lowered her gaze to the victim's throat to find heavy bruising on either side.

Then the apiarist started to cough.

He quickly backed away from the hive and retreated to the nearest open window. He leaned precariously through the unscreened opening. After a few moments, he stepped back and Elizabeth heard another echoing *crunch*. It rang out like a gong in her head, even over the rain and the buzzing bees.

He was breathing shallowly. "Look, I'm sorry. I've never used one of these things indoors before. Maybe I can use a little less smoke."

"If you need more time—"

He left the window, his clothing now damp from the rain, matching the dark circles of wetness that had grown beneath his arms. "Don't worry. I can handle this."

"Then stop screwing around and get it done."

He mock saluted her with one dry, callused hand, then turned around and disappeared back into the fog.

CHAPTER 2

Elizabeth regretted the words as soon as they were out of her mouth. The stress of the past few months was obviously getting to her.

The minute James returned, she ripped off her veil and asked him to trade places with her. High-powered flashlight in hand, she decided now would be a good time to check out the other rooms on the floor.

She started at the room closest to her. The door was wide open, having lost whatever hardware had secured it. There was so much debris scattered across the floor that it was difficult to walk. She picked her way through and shined the light on various piles. Maybe something would stand out—something that didn't look like it should be there with the rest of the crap.

It was just rubbish. Stained rags and empty paint cans, random pieces of wood, some with rusty, sharp nails poking through. Elizabeth stepped carefully, not taking any chances.

There was a bundle of old newspapers in the corner,

as yellow as ripe bananas. Workers had left empty soda cans and bottles scattered across the room.

She did the same routine in the other rooms, scanning piles of junk, stepping carefully among broken floorboards. The hotel room closest to the stairs had an old mattress in it—not one that would have been there when the floor was still accommodating guests. It was thin, stained, and looked cheaper than something you'd find in an airport Holiday Inn. If the victim had been raped, this might have been where it happened. She marked it in her notes.

Elizabeth crossed the hallway. This room was cleaner than the rest; it was as though they'd made more progress here. All of the wallpaper had been removed and the floor polished down to bare, unfinished wood.

The beam of her flashlight fell on the portrait of a woman, her glossy dark eyes staring up at Elizabeth, the photo paper reflecting dully in the fluorescent beam. She crouched and saw that it was a whole stack of pictures, with people dressed in clothing styles dating from the twenties. There were a couple of nicer shots in tarnished silver frames, the glass long since broken, long enough that the edges weren't sharp and the dust had settled in a fine layer over all the pieces.

That wasn't all.

Blood.

She marked it down as another thing for the CSU to collect, then resumed her search.

THE BEES WERE NEARLY GONE when James ushered in the crime scene technicians. They set up bright work lights around the room, illuminating the grime Elizabeth had been looking at through the darkness. It was a flash of harsh reality: back to the real world.

James had news. "I got a name for our victim. Karina Brookes."

"How did you manage that?"

"I asked the hotel manager if they'd had any unexplained disappearances, and there was an investigation a couple of weeks ago concerning a young woman who was last seen in the hotel bar. The manager had held on to the card of the detective who was handling the inquiry."

"Who was it?"

"Franklin Jones."

"Oh no," she said, shaking her head. "He's an idiot. I can't believe he hasn't been forcibly transferred yet."

James smiled. "Maybe they should send him to Bradenton. Anyway, I called the guy. He said Karina was wearing a skimpy blue dress when she went missing, just like this one. He also emailed me a picture." He pressed a few buttons on his iPhone and turned the screen toward her.

She took the phone from him, looking back and forth between the corpse and the phone. Elizabeth's eyes lingered on the area where the bottom half of the victim's face should have been. "It's hard to call it a match, under the circumstances."

"It's highly unlikely that it's not her."

She looked at the phone again. "So what did Franklin say about suspects? Was she at the bar with anyone in particular?"

He nodded enthusiastically. "She left with an older guy. Apparently, the bartender remembered the night in question pretty well. We'll have to talk to her tomorrow."

"What about Franklin? Didn't he do all this? Did he find the guy?"

"Yes and no. According to him, the place was thoroughly searched and he never figured out who the mystery man was."

"Sounds pretty sloppy."

James lowered his voice. "Either Franklin really is a complete moron, or the killer brought the body back to the hotel after it was searched. Which would make the killer a moron. Maybe they're both morons. Not that it matters, since McQuinn is probably going to take this case away from us. I'm too new and you're too...well, I hear you're not his favorite person. "

At the mention of Captain McQuinn, their homicide supervisor, Elizabeth shivered. At that very moment, he was probably asleep on the couch in front of a television blaring Your Baby Can Read infomercials while his wife played Halo on their son's PlayStation. And yet, he held the future of her career in his thick, red-mottled hand. She snapped her notebook closed and slipped it back in her pocket. "I'll figure something out."

Footsteps slowed behind them and they both turned to see the Miami-Dade medical examiner. James had a naughty-toddler expression on his face.

"You're not getting this party started without me, are you?" Dr. Kamen stepped around to the other side·of the victim.

Elizabeth quickly rose to her feet. "We were just discussing something...unrelated."

"That's the good thing about the deceased. They know how to keep their mouths shut." She got down to the victim's level, placing a serious-looking metal briefcase on the floor beside her. "Any weapons found?"

"Not yet. It doesn't appear that he used a weapon, but you're the expert."

She nodded. "The small, disc-shaped bruises around the neck and the petechiae around the eyes do suggest strangulation. The damage to the bottom half of her face, however, is peculiar. It's possible that the assailant did something gruesome to her mouth, or it could just be insect damage. I'm going to have to bring in a forensic entomologist to consult. It's definitely not consistent with the rest of her body."

"Yes, that seemed strange to us, too," James replied, gesturing to the rest of the victim's body. "The decomposition and damage isn't as bad elsewhere."

"Yes, not even close." Dr. Kamen prodded the victim's teeth with one glove-tipped finger, and it was like she'd opened the floodgates. Out spilled a mass exodus of large black ants. Where one or two of them had been lazily crawling out before, now a stream of them tumbled onto the floor.

Elizabeth stepped on the handful of them that came in her direction.

Dr. Kamen didn't even flinch. "So that's where y'all were hiding." She collected a few of them in a small plastic container and put it back into her case. Then she pulled out a large tongue depressor. "There has to be something in her mouth that's attracting them."

"A piece of gum?" James suggested.

"Definitely more than that."

As they watched, the doctor gently inserted the long, flat wooden stick into the victim's mouth. With her other hand, the doctor aimed a small penlight into the woman's mouth and leaned in closer to take a look.

Then she carefully removed the tongue depressor. Suspended from its tip, stretching down into the victim's open mouth, hung a long, viscous strand of golden slime.

"What the hell is that?" James asked, unable to hide his revulsion.

"It looks like…honey."

"From the bees? That's nuts." Elizabeth called out to the apiarist over the hum of the vacuum. "Could you please come here for a minute?"

His head snapped toward them, face shadowed by the heavy veil, then he turned off the machine. "What's wrong?"

She pointed to the victim. "She has honey in her mouth. Is that something the bees could have done?"

The apiarist took off his veil and crossed the room, gaping at the yellow goo still dripping into the corpse's mouth. He was silent for a few moments, then finally said, "No. That's not something a bee would ever do. Bees don't like death."

ELIZABETH WAS DRIVING ON AUTOPILOT, looking out the window with half-closed eyes and watching trees covered in Spanish moss fly by like ghosts.

“Not to end things on a down note,” he said, “but ‘curse of the trade’ and all that. We can probably call it a day, get a few hours of sleep, and pick things up in the morning. Awful weather for working, but perfect for sleeping.”

She felt each of her muscles relax and exhaled loudly. “I'm looking forward to some interesting dreams tonight.”

"Those bees…" He shuddered. "At least that shouldn't be a problem anymore."

"Yes, exactly. I wish I were going home, but even the hotel sounds good right now. Soft pillows, air conditioner on high..."

"Soothing music, rain lulling you into a coma, no dead bodies…"

"Maybe a couple of scented candles and a down blanket."

James sighed. "And not a moment too soon."

Elizabeth's phone rang just as she was making the turn onto US1. She looked at the screen, then at James. "It's Nick."

"Answer it."

Elizabeth slowed down and debated putting Nick on speaker, but she didn't. "What do you want?"

"I had to go to another scene after yours. I'm finding that it bears some striking similarities."

"Really? Like what?"

"You're just going to have to come down here and have a look."

"Where are you?"

"Homestead."

"*Homestead?*"

"Yes, people die out here, too."

James got the gist of the conversation just by listening to her side. "We're not going home, are we?"

"No." Elizabeth looked at the clock on the dash and then up at the street sign she'd just driven under. "It's going to take at least twenty minutes to make it out there. What exactly are you looking at?"

"The body of a young woman was found behind an abandoned house, in a *bee* yard, laid out on top of an *apiary*. The bees have made her part of their hive."

~

THE LIGHTS of multiple police cruisers lit up the old property, reflecting red and blue in the puddle spotted dirt. Elizabeth stepped through the bright beam of a CSU spotlight, squinting and raising her arm against it as she walked.

She passed a huddled group of cops who were standing closer to the service road than either the neglected house or the cordoned-off area that stretched into the wasteland behind it. Within the police tape was the bee yard. It was dotted with small white apiary boxes that reflected moonlight in their painted walls.

A uniformed officer was talking animatedly to three guys near the porch of the house, all of whom were dressed in cargo pants and jackets, their hoods pulled up against the weather.

Elizabeth pulled ahead of James, a clump of wet hair falling into her face. She brushed it aside and stepped through muddy puddles toward the slightly raised area where most of the men in blue were congregated.

The victim was splayed out on top of a white tower constructed of stacks of wooden frames. It was an apiary; a rather large one. It was one of four tucked behind the old house. Neglect was showing in the warped pieces that barely fit together with gaps throughout. One of the victim's legs dangled limply over the edge, the toes of her bare foot pointing to a crevice from which a tumult of bees spilled out. The bees had covered her body with something hard that was dark gold in color. Not honey. Something else. They'd built it into her openings, as though trying to fix her.

The woman was longer than the box, her head

dangling precariously over the side. Elizabeth made a circuit around the box to the victim's head, and came to face to face with her open eyes. Her mouth was gaping open from gravity, and her long black hair was draped over the frame walls.

Making her way around the box—thankful that the bees didn't seem aggressive—Elizabeth saw what made this case worse than the last. The woman's hands had been chopped off at the wrists.

Amputated. It might not be completely logical, considering that the woman from the crime scene before this one wouldn't be any less dead if she still possessed her hands, but it was just something Elizabeth couldn't stomach. It almost always showed a killer who didn't value the life of another human being any more than he might that of a cockroach.

She backed away, thoughts already forming. This victim had definitely died elsewhere before being moved to her final resting place. The height of the apiary combined with the awkwardness of the whole thing made her dying where she currently lay near impossible. The obvious answer was the house behind her. It was as much a part of the crime scene as the bee yard.

Before she got very far, Matt intercepted her. He seemed surprised to see her. "Oh, Stratton. How's it going? Get a look at the vic?"

"Yeah. We're looking at a killer who clearly wants to be noticed."

"Definitely."

She pointed to the front of the house. "Those guys you were talking to—are they the ones that found the body?"

"Urban explorers. Bunch of retards." He gestured to

a couple of kids—probably in their early twenties at most—sitting on the ground near the house. Then he scanned the periphery of the crime scene until his gaze alit on one more person, camera in hand, snapping pictures of the victim. "That little cocksucker," he muttered. "I told you to put that camera away! This is a crime scene, not a birthday party!"

"What about Nick?" Elizabeth said. "He go home?"

Matt chuckled. "No, he's in the house. Said there were a couple things he wanted to check out. Guy probably killed her in there, then took her outside."

"That's what I was thinking."

"I told you to drop it, jackass!" With a scowl, Matt turned away from her and stalked off toward the guy with the camera.

Though the rain had stopped, the moon was covered by gray clouds, which were bunched up like dryer lint. The old farmhouse was illuminated by the extended halos of the nearest CSU lights.

White painted paneling was peeling away from the walls to show the rot beneath. Fingers of mold crept up from the ground, snaking out of the overgrown grass. The windows above were clouded with grime, and dark, save for one that showed the sporadic glimmer of a moving flashlight.

Elizabeth stepped onto the back porch. It protested with aching groans that seemed to echo through the entire foundation.

She took a deep breath and stepped inside.

CHAPTER 3

The first thing she heard inside the house was dripping. She had walked into the kitchen. The ancient appliances were covered in a thick coat of grime. Junk had been piled on top of a small breakfast table in the corner of the room—clearly misplaced items from other parts of the house. To her surprise, there were still pots on the countertops and mason jars half-filled with god knows what lining the backsplash. Yellowed lace curtains still hung above the sink, and a dollar-store Virgin Mary candle sat undisturbed on the sill.

The floorboards creaked with each move she made. There was an almost grassy smell in the house, as though the outside had begun to creep in. Like the paneling outside, the paint covering the kitchen walls had succumbed to the relentless humidity and was hanging off in glossy waves.

"Where are you, Nick?" She pulled out her flashlight for the second—and hopefully last—time that evening.

She stepped over a warped threshold, crossing

beneath a watchful crucifix and into a living area. She bumped into a small side table and reached out with ungloved hands to steady it, cursing silently. Thanks to the urban explorers outside, the scene had already been disturbed anyway. As she steadied the table, her gaze fell onto a pale blue dish balanced on the corner, which was holding an assortment of matchbooks, spare change, and a laminated holy card picturing an elderly man. It was like the home's inhabitants had just disappeared one day. There was no movement, no sound coming from anywhere inside the house. "Nick?"

A flash of color caught her eye. It was a mustard yellow tufted armchair set beneath a small window. Its side was reflecting a bit of light from one of the CSU lamps outside, giving it a surreal glow. The floor surrounding it was covered in paint peelings, but the chair itself was clean.

Passing through the dining room and the foyer didn't yield any more clues than the kitchen and living areas had. Elizabeth looked up the unlit staircase, its top steps disappearing into the dark upper level. While she was debating, she heard the ceiling creak from a heavy footstep.

Sighing, she started up the stairs, moving her flashlight back and forth in sequence with each step. Upstairs, there was a small hall, off of which three dim rooms opened. Two of the three doors were closed. *Great.* She stood at the top of the stairs, hand lightly touching the banister. "Nick! Could you come out here, please? I'm not in the mood to search for you right now."

Silence.

"This little game you're playing isn't funny. You're

not going to scare me by jumping out of a closet, okay? Just give it up."

Tired of the game, tired of taking it slow, Elizabeth stormed through the rooms one by one, forcefully pushing open the doors, crossing mildewy wall-to-wall carpeting, and peering in small old-fashioned closets. In the second room, she paused to look at the remains of an old iron bed frame with a framed sampler that seemed to have irregular burnt edges on the wall above where the headboard should have been. She heard a noise. Probably Nick in the closet, just as she'd expected.

Shaking her head, she crept toward the door. Maybe she could turn the tables and surprise *him*. Elizabeth whipped open the door. "Ha!"

Pressed up against the back wall of the closet was a man. It wasn't Nick.

Leaping backwards with a yelp of alarm, Elizabeth's hand went to her holster. She pulled her gun and aimed it steadily at the intruder. "I want you to come out slowly, with your hands in front of your body."

The man did as she said, showing her his empty hands. "Listen, I was here with the other guys, showing them around, taking a few time delay shots during the lightning storm. I wanted to get some more pictures before the cops got here, but I got involved, and I didn't want them to see me leaving the house..."

Elizabeth shook her head and rolled her eyes. "What were you scared of? Is that your work in the backyard?"

In the corner of her eye, Elizabeth saw Nick enter the room. He hung back, not getting involved in the stand-off just yet.

"No, of course not. My name is Dave Jackson and the guys outside will vouch for me. Well, I think they will." He was blinking rapidly. "Can you put down the gun? Maybe if I show you my ID?"

Nick laughed at Dave. "Word of advice, guy? This woman is the last person you want to be facing when you reach for your wallet. At least not when she's pointing a gun at you."

Dave's eyes went wide, hand freezing mid-reach. "I'm not moving. I swear."

Elizabeth glanced at Nick over her shoulder without lowering the gun. "You always show up at just the right moment."

"It's a gift. Now, like the guy said, can you put the gun down? Unless you're afraid of him knocking you unconscious with a Nikon hard body, I think he's harmless."

She lowered her weapon. "Where were you, anyway?"

"I was downstairs. Where were you?"

"I didn't enter the house through a second story window."

They walked Dave out of the house, Elizabeth hoping the two victims were not connected. Not because she feared a serial killer was on the loose, but because if the crimes were connected, there would be no question of her handling the case with James alone. She would also have to work with Nick.

"Come back into the house with me. I want to show you something." Nick started walking, assuming her compliance.

She followed, leaving Dave to explain himself to a much less understanding police officer. The house seemed to have less personality with Nick standing in it. All he had to do was stand there—all six foot three inches of him—and the doorframes seemed to shrink.

"Back upstairs." The stairs protested at his heavily treaded, solid leather soles striking the boards like a hammer. He led her into the bedroom at the end of the short hall. "First, the bed."

A bare mattress rested on an ugly utilitarian frame. Nick was pointing his flashlight at a dark spot near the head.

"Looks like blood," she said.

"Blood and hair evidence." He turned around, left the room, and stepped inside a small bathroom. "Now look at this."

There was a small Plexiglas shelf above the sink. On it rested a toothbrush with frayed bristles, a cloudy plastic cup, and a roll of bath tissue. "The toothbrush looks pretty old, but the toilet paper is white as snow," she said.

"I think someone's been living here, or using it as a love nest. Happens a lot with these old, abandoned places. And if we can figure out who that is without scaring them off, maybe they can tell us something."

"Our closet explorer Dave said he brought those other three to show them the place. Sounds like he's been here before."

"Guess we'd better have another talk with Davey boy." Back downstairs they went, but instead of heading for the door, Nick went into the living room. He sat down in the lonely yellow chair and leaned forward, resting his elbows on his knees. "Okay, tell me what happened at the Roosevelt after I left."

She paused. "You're really going to sit there?"

"It's just an old chair."

Choosing to remain standing, she crossed her arms in front of her body, put her weight on her heels, and started talking. She described the events of the night in detail. She saved the most interesting part for last. "The crazy thing is what the ME found in the victim's mouth. Honey."

"He filled her mouth with honey?"

"Probably after death. The autopsy will tell us for sure. Being there, seeing everything—it looks like he killed her and then took the time to do all the extra stuff. I don't know for whose benefit. So now I'm wondering if the body out back also has honey in its mouth."

"She's been exposed to the elements. I don't know if we'll be able to tell one way or the other." He shook his head. "So I hear you are acquainted with an emergency beekeeper."

"He's a clumsy buffoon."

He shrugged. "I'm used to dealing with clumsy buffoons. Make sure you give Matt the details. Then maybe you can go talk to those 'urban explorer' morons. Especially our closet case."

"I'd be delighted," she said with a false smile and walked out without another word. As usual, Nick had already decided he was the boss.

Unfortunately, he was right.

CHAPTER 4

James was sitting on the porch steps, holding a can of Mountain Dew in one hand and a tin of chewing tobacco in the other, looking like he belonged there. He looked up at her, and the tobacco he'd been chewing shifted to a holding position in his left cheek. "I didn't want to interrupt."

"It wasn't a date."

He pointed to the witnesses, who were seated in the grass within shouting distance. "I think they're getting antsy."

They were in varying stages of aggravation, from what she could tell, probably depending on individual temperament. The skinny one was fiddling with his camera nonchalantly, as though he wanted to be allowed to use it. His friend with the beard was tapping his foot on the ground quickly; if it had been in sync with his heartbeat, he'd be dead. While he did that, he watched the police intently. Dave seemed to be arguing with the third one. Though their words were inaudible to Elizabeth, their gestures and facial expressions spoke volumes.

Elizabeth offered James a hand up. “Let’s take our turn speaking to them.”

He spit into the soda can, then tucked the tobacco back inside his jacket pocket. “Let’s do it.”

Elizabeth grabbed some evidence bags and a permanent marker from a CSU technician on her way over. She arrived after James.

James had already gotten the ball rolling. “So, gentleman, we have a few things we need to talk about.”

The fat, bearded one gave a big, exaggerated sigh. “We've already talked to the other detectives. We've been talking for an hour and a half at this point. I'm not sure what you think you're going to uncover that—”

“You may have spoken to them, but you haven't spoken to us,” James replied. “You may not like it, but we don't happen to like trespassers. Your cooperation right now is keeping you out of jail. Are we on the same page?”

“Fine. What do you want to know?”

James looked at Elizabeth and she stepped forward.

She gestured to Dave. “First things first—this guy with you?”

They all agreed that he was, with various synonyms of “yes.” Dave glared at her and said, “I told you. I already explained how I got separated from them.”

“Yes, of course, and we should have taken your word for it.” Elizabeth said this last part in an exaggeratedly apologetic tone. “I'm going to need your names.”

The heavy-set, irritating one said, “Paul Atreides.”

“I read that book, too. Now give me your real name.”

He raised one caterpillar eyebrow, suggesting no

one else on the scene had caught that yet, then said, "Tony Montana."

"How about everyone just pulls out their driver's license?" Elizabeth duly checked each one and jotted down the name in her notebook. The liar's name was Arnold Lofland. With a name like that, she almost forgave him for lying.

"Anyone want to give an opinion on why Dave hid in a closet instead of facing the music with the rest of you? If I were in your position, I'd be kind of annoyed that he skipped out on doing his civic duty. Why should he get out of it?"

All three of them looked blankly at her, and Arnold shrugged. "I don't know."

"You don't know?" Elizabeth noticed that one of the men—the most theatrically dressed of all of them in combat boots and camouflage cargo pants—was staring at the ground and making a line in the dirt with his heel. "What about you, Trey? What did Dave say when he left you? And how exactly did that happen? Did he stay in the house when you guys left, or did he run back into the house?"

Trey didn't look up at her. "I don't remember exactly. We were all nervous after what we'd seen. It's not often that urban explorers find bodies."

"You mean it's happened before?"

He shrugged. "I've heard stories—more in Europe, though. They have a lot of caverns over there—old caves, and unused tunnels. I think there have been a couple of times that someone got lost down there and later someone else discovered the body. That's why I never go exploring alone."

"Do you take any more precautions, like leaving

information about your whereabouts with a friend who's staying home, in case you don't return?"

He shook his head. "The group thing is enough, if you ask me. I mean, what's going to happen? The people who got into trouble in Europe...it only happened because they were alone. Getting lost is a serious danger in some places, but over here it's more a question of not getting hurt. I mean, if you're alone and fall through some rotted floor and break both your legs, who's gonna go for help?"

"Cell phone?"

"Sure, but maybe it broke in the fall. Maybe you have no reception. You need to have people with you in case you run into trouble."

She watched them all for a moment and thought back to what they had been doing before she and James had approached them. They had all been involved in their own things, like checking cameras and cell phones. "So how did this group come together tonight? Are you all friends?"

Arnold made a big, dramatic huffing noise. "What does it matter if we're friends?"

She turned to James. "I bet I know another reason why these boys don't go spelunking by themselves: it's because somebody needs to be the lookout."

"Good thinking, Stratton. I'd bet you're right."

"Because we all know that trespassing is illegal and can get you arrested."

The third guy with the serious camera equipment—Xavier —jumped up with a burst of nervous energy. It was so abrupt that Elizabeth almost went for her gun. He quickly started talking. "Hey, listen, we really didn't mean any harm. Did you mean it when you said we'd be all right if we cooperated? Because I really can't have this on my record."

He was the youngest-looking of the group—didn't really even look like a legal adult—so Elizabeth said, "It *would* look pretty bad if you were trying to get into a good college."

"I'm supposed to get the Florida scholarship, and if I screw this up, my mother—"

"Hey, buddy, calm down." James grabbed Xavier's arm. "You just need to tell us everything you know. Everything you saw. You never know what might help."

"As long as you do that, you'll stay out of trouble," Elizabeth added. "If anyone needs to worry, it's your friend Dave."

Xavier shook his head. "That's the first thing you should know. He's not our friend."

Elizabeth smiled. "Is that right?"

Arnold was playing around with his phone. Trey had gone back to drawing patterns in the dirt, and Dave was suddenly becoming very interested in what Xavier was saying. She saw James subtly put himself between Dave and Xavier. He also gestured for Dave to be quiet, and he seemed to know he was on eggshells, because he complied.

"He's a poster on an Internet forum we're all members of," Xavier said. "He's like one of the top posters there, been around since the beginning."

"And how did you all end up here tonight?"

"Dave put out the word that since he was new to Miami, he wanted to see what the rest of us considered the best sites. Said he'd been to a lot of places himself in the space of a couple months, but he wanted something new. We took him to a couple places last night—"

"Like where?"

"An old arena on Brickell, and this mansion out in the boonies. It's incredible and really untouched 'cause not many people know about it. They say it used to belong to one of the nephews of Osama Bin Laden."

"How did you decide where you were going tonight?"

"Dave told us about it. You have to understand the culture of urban exploration. There are places that only certain cliques know about, and they aren't good at sharing information. This place was one of them, and since so few people know about it, it's remained a great spot. Relatively untouched."

Arnold cursed under his breath. "We should have known better than to come here. I heard it was condemned."

Elizabeth was glad to see that the guy was opening up, but she still directed her next question at Xavier. "How did you find the body?"

"We'd actually been all through the house before we checked out the backyard, which is a good thing, because I don't think I would have gone in there if I had known about the body in the backyard."

"I'm assuming you got a lot of great pictures?"

"You're going to want them, aren't you?"

Arnold groaned and hung his head between his legs.

"Yes, I'm going to need your SD cards. If you give me correct addresses for each of you, I'll make sure you get them back."

They each pulled their cameras out and removed the memory cards. Arnold had his in his hand. "I doubt this is legal. We don't live in a police state. Our pictures belong to us."

Elizabeth kept holding out her hand, her face impassive. "Would you like to be indicted for hampering a police investigation? How about for withholding evidence?"

"Whatever." He dropped the card into her hand.

Xavier and Trey produced similar cards, and Elizabeth pulled out the evidence bags she'd gotten from the CSU tech. She dropped each card into its own bag and wrote the camera owner's name on the plastic with a black Sharpie. Dave was the last one to hand over a card, which he had removed from a camera in his large camera case.

Elizabeth looked at the canvas case, and then the size of Dave's camera. "You have another camera in there, don't you?"

"He brought two cameras with him," Xavier said.

"Thanks a lot, dude," Dave said and removed the second camera from its case and gave her the accompanying memory card.

Elizabeth turned back to Xavier. "Okay, so how did you get separated from Dave?"

Xavier looked at Dave almost apologetically, then said, "We were leaving the house, actually on the front lawn, when we saw the headlights. It was the cop who was responding to the call. He got here a whole lot faster than we expected."

"You were leaving, right? You guys weren't going to stick around."

Xavier sighed. "No, we weren't. We were all afraid. I can't speak for the rest of the guys, but I've seen a lot of movies, and this is exactly the kind of scenario where the innocent people get something pinned on them thanks to being in the wrong place at the wrong time."

Elizabeth was shaking her head. "So you were all planning on getting out of here until you realized it was too late. And Dave?"

"I guess he wasn't accepting that it was too late. He said he was going to hide in the house until everyone was gone. I told him he was crazy. I've seen *Law & Order*. I figured he'd be hiding all night. I told him it wasn't worth it."

"And he said?"

"That he had a warrant out for his arrest."

"Okay, that's not true," Dave said with a healthy amount of indignation. "I was just lying for their sake. I've never been in trouble in my life."

"I don't know, son," James said. "It sounds pretty plausible. Frankly, it actually makes you look better. A little more normal, if you know what I mean."

"Yeah, well, it's still not true."

"Don't worry. We can find out really quickly if you have a warrant out for your arrest or not."

"I want each of you to make an appointment with the medical examiner's office." Elizabeth gave them a piece of paper with the details. "We need fingerprints and DNA swabs. Don't even think of getting a lawyer involved to try to get out of doing it, or we'll book you all on trespassing charges."

She saw Nick approach in her peripheral vision. It was never difficult to see him coming. It was all in his swagger. He was one of those detectives who looked the part, stretching his salary at discount stores so he could wear Zegna and Hugo Boss, but he could have been wearing jeans and anyone with the gift of sight would still know that he was in charge. He kept his distance, but signaled her.

"Don't let me down," she said, and they left the creepers to argue amongst themselves.

Nick was giving the group the side eye as he told her in a low voice, "I had an idea that maybe Dave had a good reason for hiding. So I checked to see if there were any warrants out for him."

"And?"

"He's not even in the system."

Elizabeth bit her lip. "He wasn't counting on me finding him, obviously. He didn't want his name on the record."

"Yeah, but there's no way he could have expected the other three guys to keep their mouths shut."

"Apparently he's not too bright." She looked around the yard to see who was still working. She saw Matt and decided she needed some more information. James followed, and Nick stayed behind to babysit the witnesses.

"Hey, Matt, got a minute? Out of curiosity, did you come on aggressively to those kids?"

"Is that what they said?"

"No, this is purely for my own edification. There's something I'm trying to figure out."

Matt leaned back on his heels. "I might have been preparing a little lecture on my way here about respecting private property, but it didn't turn out the way I expected. When we parked in front of the house, those kids came out to greet us. They must have seen the lights. Before I could even get a word out of my mouth, they said, 'We were just looking around.'"

"And then they showed you the body."

"Yeah. I took one look at the victim, then told those *pendujos* to sit tight because they'd probably be wanted for questioning. Then I called it in."

"Did you walk through the house?"

"Nah, figured that was up to the detectives."

"Were you doing any kind of exploring?"

"Nope. Me and Tim, we're pros at standing around, and that's exactly what we did. We stood here and guarded the crime scene until Fiorello got here."

"Thanks, Matt." Elizabeth walked away, James moving quietly beside her.

Finally, he said, "Interesting line of questioning. Where are you going with this?"

"I don't know about that Dave guy. Obviously he's not lying about coming with the rest of the group, but hiding in the closet was a really creepy thing to do. Judging from what Matt just said, the guy had ample time to sneak out of here. It was some time before the entire cavalry arrived. He could have slipped out unnoticed."

"You can't always explain fear. At the time, maybe the closet felt like the safest place to be."

"Out of all of them, he seemed the least disturbed by their gruesome discovery."

"So you're wondering if he could be our guy."

"It's possible. I mean, you set up something like this, you want to see people's reactions. Who knows if he was in that closet the whole time, or if he just hid in there when he heard me coming?" Her eyes went wide. "Actually, I heard footsteps on the second floor. At the time, I thought it was Nick, but Nick was downstairs. Dave could have been watching us through an upstairs window."

"Sounds pretty creepy to me," James said.

Elizabeth gazed at the abandoned farm house. "I'm thinking there's enough dust in that place that we should be able to find his footprints in any room he went into."

The lump of chew in James's cheek moved from one side to the other. "You're right, Stratton. Sounds like a CSU job. Me? I'm late for an appointment with my bed."

CHAPTER 5

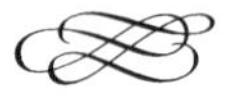

Captain McQuinn was standing in front of his desk, looking more ready for action than Elizabeth had ever seen him. He might as well have had boxing gloves on, because he looked like he was ready for a fight. "So let me get this straight: we have two dead women, both found with their mouths full of honey."

"That's the status as of this moment," Nick said. He had decided to join Elizabeth and James in the meeting at the last minute, even though he'd already copied the captain on his recommendations. "It wasn't as obvious with the second body, but Dr. Kamen confirmed it this morning."

"And you want me to put Stratton and Faraday on this? Untested amateurs?"

Elizabeth shook her head. "I've been on the force for more than ten years, and James has twenty years of experience. The fact that he was in a different department doesn't make him a rookie any more than I am."

"Miami isn't a regular city. It might as well be a

whole other country, considering how differently everything operates down here."

"Well, I absolutely cannot disagree with you on that point." And she wouldn't. After all, at times she wondered why she hadn't transferred out to somewhere quieter. But as foreign as Miami was compared to other parts of the US, it was home. "You have to give us a chance at some point. Now's as good a time as any."

The captain shook his head. "I don't know about that. This case has the potential to be huge. What if there are more bodies out there?"

"Then you'll need as many detectives working this as you can get, and these two will be working the case anyway," Nick said. "What are you afraid of?"

McQuinn nodded to Elizabeth.

"I was cleared for work," she said. "The counselor didn't see any reason why I couldn't resume my duties."

Nick stared ahead, past the captain's desk and through the window that fronted a courtyard. "You're also making things difficult for Faraday, McQuinn. The fact that he's from Bradenton would normally be off your radar. You're just looking for something to hold against him."

"And why would I do that?" In contrast to Nick, McQuinn had started moving, stalking around the office like a feral cat.

"All because of Elizabeth."

The captain didn't meet her gaze or that of anyone else in the room.

Elizabeth started to open her mouth, but quickly snapped it shut.

"Admit it. You don't want *her* back in the rotation; it has nothing to do with James."

McQuinn shrugged. "What do you want me to say, Fiorello?"

"It's not so much what I want you to say. I want you to realize that what I say is true, and realize that it's monumentally unfair to Faraday."

So this was Nick's way of putting in a good word for her. Agreeing that she was a mess, but that James should get a chance.

James fiddled with the zipper on his windbreaker. "I appreciate the thought, but you don't need to fight on my behalf. I like to think that Elizabeth and I come as a team."

Nick continued. "You have to have faith in Faraday. I think if Elizabeth does lose her way, he can keep her in check."

At this, both Nick and McQuinn burst out laughing. McQuinn finally said, once he caught his breath, "As if anyone is capable of that."

"The bottom line," Nick continued, "is that you need to stop penalizing Faraday for the partner you gave him."

Seeing that this line of defense had a chance of working, Elizabeth still didn't interrupt. She watched the captain think, adjusting the position of a couple of different photos on his desk.

Finally, he turned around and said to Nick, "And I suppose I should make you the lead on the case, which would be even more of a failsafe."

Elizabeth gritted her teeth. That was one way to punish her.

Nick looked more than pleased with himself. "Yes, I can be lead on this. I'm going to give them a lot of freedom though. I won't be their nanny."

Captain McQuinn shrugged and said, "All right. I might as well go for it. If this goes horribly wrong, you know who I'll be looking at."

Nick nodded as though he understood. "Now that that's taken care of, let's go catch a bad guy."

NICK LEFT QUICKLY, saying he'd call them when the medical examiner was finished with the two bodies. He'd gotten Kamen to prioritize them. If the two crimes scenes were connected, the situation was more serious than if they were unrelated. They were, of course, operating under a lot of assumptions, but one could never underestimate the importance of instinct.

Elizabeth dragged her feet back to the cubicle she and James would now share, not exactly feeling like Bruce Willis in *Armageddon*. She wasn't even Ben Affleck. She slumped in her chair and aimlessly pushed around some paperwork for a few seconds before picking up a pen and poising it above the paper.

"Paperwork, huh?" James said, leaning against the desk. He pulled a tin of tobacco out of his pocket and rolled it around in his hand.

"Might as well."

He responded with a low, throaty chuckle.

"Oh come on, James. It has to get done."

"We both know that you're still smarting from that meeting we just walked out of. You know, the one where Nick made himself the star?"

She perked up, pushing the rolling chair away from the desk and looking up at him. "Isn't he just the most aggravating son-of-a-bitch you've ever met?"

"You could say that. He's arrogant and he doesn't even try to cover it up. The guy is very proud of himself."

"Exactly!" Elizabeth looked at him, sighed, then said, "But you look happy about something."

He nodded. "The approach that Nick took in there didn't make you look very good, but it didn't make you look worse, either. The captain has his opinion—which, from what I've gathered around the department, isn't the prevailing one around here. You have a lot of people on your side, and I wouldn't be surprised if Nick was one of them."

"But he said—"

"It doesn't matter what he said. He guessed correctly that by using me as the experienced detective who's been unfairly penalized, McQuinn would be guilted into letting me work. And the only way to get me back to work is by including you. This all has more to do with the captain's perceptions than Nick's, or anyone else's."

"Whatever."

"The bottom line is, we're back in the game. Running with the big boys. " He pounded on the desk behind him. "Who cares what anyone thinks? We'll make them eat their words."

She blinked a few times until the blur left her eyes. Her heart beat faster and an excitement she hadn't felt in months flooded her body. She stood up. "You're right. We'll make them look like the Keystone cops. You ready to get to work?"

He nodded. "That's what I'm talking about! We'll hit up the Roosevelt and talk to that bartender. Then we can pay a visit to our friendly neighborhood medical examiner. Damn if that woman isn't the hottest doctor I've ever had."

"She's not *your* doctor, James. She cuts up dead people."

"And she does it with a smile." He finally gave up the fight and popped open the Skoal can. Pushing a wad into the corner of his mouth, he said, "This is great. I don't know about you, Elizabeth, but I'm happier than a pig in shit."

"KARINA, you say her name was? Yeah, I remember her. She'd be hard to forget." Linda, the bartender at the Roosevelt hotel, looked like the kind of woman you could pour your heart out to. The entire bar had that kind of feel of comfortable hominess characterized by dim lighting, pockmarked tables, and a wide variety of cardboard coasters scattered across every surface.

"What made her unforgettable?" James seemed more comfortable in bars than he was in most places.

"The way she was dressed was the first thing. Beautiful girl with a body to match, but that dress she had on made her stand out in here. This is the kind of place where most people just stumble in after work without changing, even on a Friday night."

"The famous Roosevelt Hotel isn't what it used to be."

"Yep. Those days are long gone." As Linda spoke, she poured shots and highballs with the precision of a computer. Elizabeth watched her pour three glasses of scotch and, despite moving quickly and not using any measuring tools, the volume in all three were identical.

Elizabeth tapped her foot on the bottom rung of the

barstool. "And you told the detective who was investigating her disappearance that she came in alone?"

"Yes, but she wasn't alone for long."

James was entering notes into his phone. "Before we ask you about her mystery man: you said the way she was dressed was just the first thing you remember about her. What else made her memorable?"

"She was drunk. I mean, the girl was acting very night-at-the-truck-stop tacky." Her eyes fell. "I hope you don't think I lack sympathy for the whole thing. I can't believe someone killed her. And right after I saw her, no less."

"It's an awful thing, that's for sure," Elizabeth said.

"It freaks me out to think that I might have made a drink for a murderer." She wiped down the bar with a pale blue rag, her face pensive. "So, the guy she left with…I suppose the other detectives never found him?"

"Unfortunately, no. We'd like to know whatever you told them. Maybe we'll have better luck."

"Absolutely." After popping open a Heineken for a guy at the other end of the bar, she sidled back over. "She wasn't in here very long before this older guy made his move. He was in his forties, at least."

"Attractive?"

"He was no Matthew McConaughey, but he wasn't bad looking."

"And—well, I guess I already know the answer to this since Franklin would have already gone down this path—but did he pay with a credit card?"

Linda gave her a wry grin. "Nope. He paid me by pulling out a big ole wad of cash and peeling a few bills off of it. Made up some dumb story about not trusting credit cards. Like I'm going to swipe it through a card reader under the bar or something."

Elizabeth slumped forward in the bar stool, wishing she could get a glass of something strong and straight up. "Had he been in here before or has he been since?"

"No and no." Linda turned to the side, looking at the guy she'd brought the beer to. "I think he might have spoken to Max a bit. I thought about it last night after the manager let me know what was going on. I was trying to remember everything I could."

Elizabeth looked at the guy and he gave her a friendly nod.

"He's a regular." She called the guy over and he moved to a closer stool. After he was settled, his beer placed on the Rolling Rock coaster in front of him, Linda said, "These detectives want to ask you a couple of questions."

"About?"

Since Linda seemed to have an easy way with him, Elizabeth nodded for her to continue.

"There was a woman who came in here a couple of weeks ago. Sexy blue dress, drunk off her ass. Do you remember her?"

He smiled, showing clean white teeth. He looked a little young to be wasting his life away on a barstool. "That was the most entertaining thing to happen here in months."

"I know, right?" Linda frowned. "Unfortunately, someone killed her that night, and these detectives are trying to figure out who did it. I've been trying to help them by telling them everything I remember."

He took a swig of his beer. "And you're wondering if I might also remember something useful?"

"Exactly."

Max rested his jaw on his fist for a moment, then

looked directly at Elizabeth. “I know she left with some guy. It didn’t take long.”

“Do you have any idea who he was?”

He shook his head. “I actually spoke to him a bit. Out in the lobby, he asked me if this was a good place to get a drink. I told him it was, and he followed me in. We just talked for a few more minutes about…I think it was the last hurricane? I never caught his name.”

Linda pursed her lips.

James took care of the next part of the routine, turning on the good old boy charm. "Linda, do you think you could do us a solid? I'm going to leave this card here with my name and number, and if that guy ever walks in here again, can you call me immediately?"

"Sure thing. I'd be happy to help." She seemed to study him for a moment, her eyes narrowing as though she were looking at a far off place. "You know, you look kind of familiar. You ever been to a cop joint up in Bradenton?"

James's eyes went wide. "The Rusty Barnacle?"

"That's the one. I used to pull night shifts there a few nights a week while my mom stayed over with the baby."

"Small world! What made you move down here?"

"The weather. Those extra ten degrees really make a difference." She shook her head. “And, well, my mother passed, and I needed the change of scenery. Just me and the kid now.”

“I'm sorry to hear that.”

“Thanks,” Linda said, and she smiled at him across the bar for a moment before she was called away to provide another beer for another lonely customer.

James hooked the heel of his shoe on to the bar stool rung and turned toward Elizabeth. “I think I'll finish up the paperwork here, if you don't mind collecting the security footage by yourself?"

"Yeah, yeah, yeah," she said with a grin. "You deserve a break. 'Age before beauty,' right?"

"Get out of here," he said and pushed her to the exit.

CHAPTER 6

Elizabeth found the security room, but the main desk was empty. She finally found one of the security guards partially leaning out an open door. She stood behind him and cleared her throat.

He spun around, tossing a cigarette outside before acknowledging her. “Can I help you?”

She showed him some ID and explained what was going on.

He introduced himself as Tim Barnes. He'd already heard about the body being found in the hotel and was eager to help. “I know you're going to need the security footage.”

"Before we get to that, I wanted to ask you about something. Your general manager told me background checks are done on all employees. Are you in charge of that?"

"No, an outside company does it."

"Are they pretty reliable?"

Barnes made a little face that spoke volumes. "I don't know of any serial killers working here."

"But?"

He looked at his supervisor's office. "I don't want to spread tales."

"If it's not important to my investigation, it goes no further than me."

"Half the people working here have been to jail, and some are even still on parole. They all sit around at lunch comparing stories. *What joint were you at? How long? What'd they get you for?"*

"So the background check company is letting a lot of stuff slip through the cracks?"

"I have no idea what their criteria are. Maybe they are okay with the lesser offenses? Like I said, I don't know of anyone who's done something scary."

"That was going to be my next question."

"Definitely nothing like that."

"Okay, so the security tapes?"

"Right this way," Barnes said, leading her down a dark corridor. "We've been pretty thorough with the system. You can't get into or out of any room without being caught on tape, unless you scale the side of the building." He smiled. "Which has been done, by the way."

"Here?"

"No, on some high rise condos. I saw it on the news a few years ago. They called him Spiderman."

She smiled. "Those reporters sure love their nicknames."

"Makes it easier to keep track of people. Better than Suspect Twenty-Six."

"I guess you have a point there. You ever think of becoming a cop?"

"No way. I value my life too much, and I have a tendency towards clinical depression. No offense." He looked away and then looked back hesitantly. "Isn't it sad seeing dead bodies all the time? I mean, those are people, people that somebody loves. People that somebody gave birth to."

"Sad as it is, people are going to die whether I'm there to see the aftermath or not. Every time I catch a bad guy, I wonder who he might have killed if he had been allowed to go free."

"He might not have gone free. Someone else could have caught him."

"Why pass the buck?" She smiled.

He picked up the box of security tapes. "When you put it like that, I guess it makes sense. It's so dangerous though..."

"It's more dangerous to deliver pizzas."

"And the depression..."

"More dentists kill themselves than detectives."

“Maybe you should have been in sales.” Barnes looked around. “Do you have a car you want me to carry these to for you?"

"That would be great."

She found James along the way. As soon as they were back in the car, James tucked the paperwork into a folder and buckled himself in. "Where to now?"

“How could you forget? We’re going to the happiest place on Earth: the morgue."

IT WAS APPROPRIATELY cold in the medical examiner's office, too cold for the slightly damp cardigan she'd grabbed from the floor of James's disastrously messy car. With the weather they'd been having, it was hard to ever feel dry, but at least it was usually warm. Like a fog-filled bathroom. Her voice echoed conspicuously when she greeted Dr. Kamen, as if she were disturbing the silence of a library.

Elizabeth exchanged a glance with James before asking, "Did Nick make it here yet?"

"He just stepped out to grab some coffee. Long night, from what I understand."Elizabeth walked closer to the doctor, giving a wide arc to the body exposed on the table, recognizing the woman she'd first seen with the backdrop of a few thousand buzzing bees. The lower half of her face was still missing, but under the bright fluorescent lights and in the clinical setting, she almost didn't look real. Like a naked mannequin.

Dr. Kamen leaned forward conspiratorially. "So you're back in the rotation, eh?"

Elizabeth nodded. "As of this morning."

"I would say knock 'em dead, but I guess you're striving for the opposite."

Nick walked in with his usual stride. "Great, you're here. I tried not to ask many questions so Dr. Kamen wouldn't have to repeat herself."

James was standing at the head of the victim. "So, Dr. Kamen, are you much of a drinker? If I had your job, I'd sure drink."

"That's not the kind of question I was thinking of," Nick said.

Dr. Kamen, ignoring Nick, said, "I love a great Cabernet. And please call me Jane."

"Of course," he said with a sly wink.

"I know it's difficult not to be flirtatious in such a romantic setting," Nick said, "but can we get this show on the road?"

Dr. Kamen pulled on a pair of fresh latex gloves

with a brisk *snap*. "You've got to stop being so uptight, Nick. I feel sorry for your poor mother."

"I feel sorry for his girlfriend," Elizabeth said.

Nick grimaced. "No more girlfriend. She moved out a month ago."

"There you go," the doctor said. "Finally something to explain the bad mood. Okay, let's start with Karina Brookes."

Elizabeth focused on Dr. Kamen's face rather than the victim's body. "Was she raped?"

"Yes, she was. Very aggressively, too, based on the amount of tearing I found."

"So if she did go upstairs willingly with the mystery suitor, it turned violent before they had sex," Nick said. "She changed her mind, maybe?"

"Is it possible they just had rough sex?" Elizabeth asked. "I mean, they met in a bar, they'd both been drinking..."

"It was bad enough to cause tearing. She didn't have any Rohypnol in her system, so he didn't drug her into unconsciousness. All she had in her stomach was alcohol, alcohol, and more alcohol. It may have started consensually."

"What else?" James asked.

"He was violent with her." She pointed out some bruises on Karina's thighs and arms. "She was alive longer than I would have expected, so he took his time and enjoyed himself. I found fibers in her mouth from a rag with traces of paint on it, so he seemed to have silenced her with something he found at the scene. Then he strangled her, as I first surmised. All the signs are there. Big hands, so all things point to the killer being a man."

"What have you determined about the honey?"

She turned around and picked up a test tube filled with golden goo. "There was a lot in there. It wasn't just a casual drizzle. This is a sample from her mouth. It doesn't seem like the average stuff you can buy at Publix, but hey, it's been in a decaying body for weeks. Maybe it *is* run of the mill stuff."

Elizabeth nodded. "I'm going to assume it's more unique than that. If only for the reason that I can't wrap my mind around a homicidal psychopath straddling our victim and squeezing out honey from a little bear into her mouth."

"Was she already dead when he filled her up?" James asked.

"Without a doubt."

"Have you ever seen this before? Honey in a victim's mouth?"

"No. It's pretty rare for a killer to leave *anything* behind intentionally." Dr. Kamen placed the test tube of honey in an outgoing tray next to another test tube with similar looking contents. "The lab's going to do a full workup, see if there is anything special about the sample. It will take some time."

"Okay, so what about victim number two?"

"Ah, yes. I did that autopsy first. Would you like me to bring her out?"

"No, that's all right," Elizabeth answered first, before the men. "Do you think they're victims of the same man?"

Dr. Jane Kamen stepped away from Karina's body and picked up a clipboard with notes on it. "My opinion would be that they are. Miss Doe had honey in her mouth, as well. What's more, they are both women in their twenties, with dark hair and eyes. And both were strangled and raped."

“Was Jane Doe moved?”

“Yes. She was also kept alive longer than the first victim. Possibly for more than a day. Then he cut her hands off, which was surely an attempt to prevent us from identifying her quickly.”

Shuddering, Elizabeth tried not to think too long about what the victim's last day on Earth must have been like.

Elizabeth was relieved when they finally left, parting from Nick, who had another case to discuss with the doctor. She delighted in the light shower that had started, breathing the fresh air in deeply. Working in a morgue was one job she could never have.

She picked up her pace, the rain bringing life back into her bones. "I would think the honey meant something to the killer. Why else would he do it? Nick probably wouldn't agree, but I think we should collect as many different brands of honey as we can. Then maybe the lab can match it and possibly narrow it down to a specific store.”

"Already going against the grain,” he said. “You're going to get me fired, aren't you?"

"I'll get you fired, excommunicated, and deported," she told him.

He spit a dark wad into his cup. "Let's get started, then."

~

THE VULTURE POUNCED on her as soon as they rounded the corner of the building. "Ms. Stratton? Can I ask you a few questions?"

Elizabeth backed away from the microphone thrust

into her face and blinked against the bright light the cameraman was holding. "No comment."

"We've been told that there are already two bodies that can be attributed to The Beekeeper."

"The Beekeeper?"

"The apiary murderer?" She walked at Elizabeth's side. "Is he a serial killer?"

"There's nothing to link the two crimes at this time."

"You're suggesting it's a *coincidence* that they both had honey in their mouths?"

Elizabeth froze. That was the detail they were keeping out of the press. How did she know? "I don't know what you're talking about."

"Come on, Detective. We've got a potential serial killer on our hands with an affinity for bees and honey. The public deserves to know what to be wary of."

Elizabeth nodded. "I'd stay away from Winnie-the-Pooh."

"Are you guaranteeing a capture?"

James piped up for that one. "We'll get him. Rest assured that the police are doing everything they can to catch this killer."

"Would you label him a signature killer?"

Elizabeth opened her car door. "That's an overused term, and not relevant to this investigation."

"Thank you for your time," the reporter said.

Elizabeth leaned back in the seat and sighed. "I'm starting to think the captain wasn't doing us a favor by giving us this case."

THEY PERSONALLY DROPPED off the security footage at the tech department, explaining exactly what to look for. Elizabeth had confidence that if there were anything to find, they would find it. They had already printed many of the pictures that the urban exploring group had taken of the farm house. She and James each grabbed a stack and started leafing through them.

There were a lot of pictures of empty rooms, lonely chairs, broken furniture, and peeling paint.

The tech guy watched her go through them. "You looking for anything in particular?"

Elizabeth shrugged. "It's sort of a combination between 'I'll know it when I see it' and just keeping an eye out for anything that could be important later. I'm familiarizing myself with what they saw, since they were—we have to assume—the first people to come upon the crime scene."

Rising from his chair, the tech guy walked over to the printer and offered her another stack. "These latest ones will probably interest you."

The minute she saw the photos, she called James over. "Take a look at this."

Instead of the abandoned house, these were pictures of the victim. There were pictures of the apiary with the body lying on top of it, and close-ups of the victim's arm, which ended at the wrist in a raw stump. Elizabeth was in many of them, studying the dead woman in front of her, jacket blowing in the wind, wet hair stuck to her face. There were a few pictures where Elizabeth was actually the main subject, her body in sharp focus, the corpse artistically blurred.

She didn't like these pictures. Crime scene photographs were usually gritty and detailed. It was very odd to see the victim in images that looked like they belonged in a museum exhibit.

"Wow," James said. "Who's the photographer?"

"I'll give you one guess." Elizabeth double-checked the records to be sure. "Dave took these."

"So he thinks someone's tragic death is an opportunity to audition for Art Basel?" He pulled his phone out of his pocket. "We need to put a rush on that DNA testing."

THE BEE YARD was dotted with white hive boxes that, from a distance, looked like graves. The farmer approached them, shaking his head in disgust. In the past, he'd been paid good money to rent out small parcels of his land to local beekeepers. They'd even offered him some of their sweet honey. This was different. Some rogue beekeeper had planted their bees on his land without his permission, hoping that with all the acres he had to supervise, he wouldn't notice. And what's worse, that same person had abandoned the apiary completely and allowed it to expand wildly.

He stuffed some fuel in the bottom of a smoker and lit it with an old Zippo. It quickly took and filled the air with smoke, which he directed at the bees. He knew a thing or two about bees. He didn't need some overpriced exterminator to take care of them when he could do it himself.

Dressed in white from head to toe, he walked up to the first hive box in a row of six. The bees were clustered together on the outside of the box. The farmer looked up at the dark sky, which was heavy with clouds. The coming storm would send the bees scrambling for shelter, shivering within the wood frames with furiously beating wings. They were content to take in the fresh air for now.

He lifted the top panel of the box and carefully propped it on the ground. When he looked inside and lifted the first frame, he wasn't surprised to see that the colony wasn't thriving. It was hard enough to get a good colony going when it was being monitored. He was surprised by the amount of hard, sticky resin covering the frame and running in rivulets down to the bottom of the box.

He propped the frame against the hive on the ground. He leaned over the box and looked into the space left behind by the frame. There seemed to be a frame missing besides the one he'd just taken out. In the empty space, an extra honeycomb had grown asymmetrically. Using a pair of long tongs, he removed as much of the comb as he could, then peered into the dark depths of the box.

There was a lump in the bottom, completely covered in propolis. He nodded to himself knowingly. A mouse had gotten into the hive. It would have quickly been stung to death by the drones and then, as the mouse was too heavy to be removed from the hive, the bees would have completely covered it in propolis. The corpse would have essentially been mummified.

He reached farther into the box, gripped the hard lump with his tongs, then yanked it out. What had looked to be a small lump was bigger than he had expected. He lifted it into the air to take a good look at it, turning it slowly from side to side.

That was no mouse.

He dropped the object back into the box, disturbing the perfectly constructed comb. The angry buzzing in his ears dulled to a barely perceptible hum as he stared into the gap, torn between fascination and disgust.

It was a human hand.

THE REST of James and Elizabeth's evening was spent visiting every supermarket, convenience store, and bodega surrounding the crime scenes. They bought every brand of honey they saw, depositing each in the backseat of the car.

Sometimes they hit pay dirt, picking up five different brands from the same store, but sometimes there was no honey to be found. She took careful notes of where she had bought each container, attaching evidence labels to each one.

Elizabeth tried to make more room in the back seat for the honey, turning to James when she was unsuccessful. "This is ridiculous. You need to clean your car."

"*Our* car," he said.

"I think not." She found a plastic bag on the floor behind the passenger seat with only a Walgreen's receipt inside, and starting filling it with everything in James's backseat. There were old newspapers, empty quarter pounder boxes, and a full—but warm—bottle of Mountain Dew. She filled the bag, then took it to the trashcan outside of the Food Lion they'd just left. Then she filled an old t-shirt with the items that weren't garbage—a few CD-Rs, two travel mugs, and a hardback copy of *Love in the Time of Cholera,* among other things—then told James to pop the trunk.

As soon as she faced the trunk, she realized her mistake. The trunk was also stuffed with clutter. She sighed as James joined her behind the car.

"I came to help," he said, dumping an armful of items into the messy trunk.

Elizabeth placed the things she found to one side,

then shifted a few rolled up posters to reveal an unfurled yoga mat. "Seriously, James?"

"That's Sophia's."

Then she pointed to a box of paperback romance novels.

"Sophia's, too. I was supposed to take them to Goodwill, but I've been too busy."

Elizabeth shook her head. "You can't blame those gas masks on your daughter, too."

"Those are just in case we have to bust someone in a suspected meth lab. You can never be too careful."

"And this?" she said, holding up a dull reproduction-medieval short sword.

"Oh, I just thought that was really cool. I need to take that home."

After five more minutes, they'd completely emptied the car's contents into the trunk. Then Elizabeth carefully lined up the honey samples on the wonderfully empty backseat. "How much nicer is that?"

"I don't know. You threw my CDs back there, too. What if I want to listen to the Mariah Carey CD my daughter burned for me?"

"I think you'll live."

CHAPTER 7

She showed up at the police lab with four-dozen different brands of honey, and lugged them up to the third floor by herself, leaving James to wait in the car.

"Delivery for Alan Finley." Elizabeth knocked on the door with the tip of her boot, hoping Alan had the good sense to open the door.

He did. "Elizabeth!"

She smiled and walked into the room with her offerings, setting them down on the first table she saw. Aside from the honey, she'd brought a full dozen Krispy Kreme donuts and two venti white mochas from Starbucks. Alan would drink them both before they cooled down. Good thing she'd finished her own latte in the car, or he would have claimed that, too. "I've come bearing bribes. With this sugar high, you're not going to come down until Friday."

"Not true," he said, shaking his head sadly. "I have a chemical imbalance that is only appeased with sugar. I have to have a constant flow. This will only last me the night."

She sat on the edge of a long, silver table. "So can you help?"

"What is it this time?"

"You probably already have the honey samples."

"The ones that were found in the mouths of two dead women?"

"That's right. Do you have any other honey on hand?"

"Only for my Darjeeling," he said with a laugh, then shook his head. "No, not even that. Tea is for quitters."

If only she could be so glib about her junk food intake. Since she'd turned thirty, it had gotten harder to eat like a college student and maintain a fit body. Alan, on the other hand, could stand to gain ten pounds. Elizabeth showed him the box of honey she'd lugged upstairs. "I want to know where he got the honey. So I collected every brand of honey I could find. It could come in handy to know whether he prefers Clove or Orange Blossom."

Alan started to sort through the box. "Honey *can* be a very specific thing. Even among one particular brand, each batch will be different. Although the bigger the company, the bigger the batches. Sometimes combined from multiple sources." Alan grabbed a glazed chocolate iced donut. "So we might be getting in over our heads."

"'We?'"

"Come on, you knew I was going to help you. Stop acting so modest. I've been helping you since I let you cheat off me during the AP Chemistry final."

"You had to bring that up." She stole one of his donuts and took a satisfying, stress relieving bite. "I made it up to you. Remember the backstage passes my dad got us to Pearl Jam?"

"All right, you win."

She smiled knowingly, then segued back to her new obsession. "So it sounds like you actually know a few things about honey."

"One of my friends from FSU is a forensic botanist. His thesis was on tracking honey pollination sources. It was really fascinating. Never helped him get laid, but fascinating."

"Did you keep in touch?"

"Just Facebook, these days."

The clock on the wall read midnight. "Thank you so much for doing this, Alan."

"Anytime, Elizabeth. Next time, drop by just to say hello. Or, better yet, we can have dinner." He certainly had more confidence than he used to. She should have expected that he would have matured since high school, but it was still surprising. She wondered how she had changed.

Back in the car, James wanted the details, and she succinctly filled him in. "He's going to prioritize the testing, possibly even stay late to get it done tonight."

James shook his head while smiling. "You've got skills, Stratton."

"Like I told you on the way here, we're old friends."

THE MANILA ENVELOPE was waiting for her when she got to her house that night. The damage her home had sustained during the hurricane had made the place unlivable for the past two weeks, but she'd gotten good news about the renovation progress earlier that day.

Aside from the need for new paint and a couple of window screens, it was good to go.

After being away for so long, it didn't surprise her that some mail had piled up. But Elizabeth didn't know why an unaddressed envelope had been shoved beneath the door.

She bolted the door and walked into the living room as she opened the envelope. Inside was a black and white picture of Elizabeth at the second crime scene. She was standing next to the backyard apiary and looking at the victim.

She quickly flipped through the pictures. They were all from the same set. Elizabeth, gazing into the distance as though contemplating life, her Burberry coat picked up by the wind to wrap around her legs. Close-ups of her looking pensive, with the body of the young woman artistically blurred behind her.

Elizabeth gripped the sheets tightly. The pictures had been taken by none other than Dave Jackson. These were the same ones she'd already copied at the station. They were from his memory card, the one she'd taken from him at the scene. How could he possibly still have access? She cursed aloud and pulled her phone out of her jacket pocket, still squeezing the pictures in her other hand. She dialed James, knowing he'd be pissed at having his rest cut short yet again, but it was time to talk to Dave. And she sure as hell wasn't going to see him alone. Not after this.

Dave was going to have to explain *how* he still had the pictures, *where* he found her home address, and *why* he giving her gruesome pictures as though they were a present.

~

THEY BANGED on Dave's door until a hairy guy wearing only pajama bottoms opened up, blinking at them with bloodshot eyes.

"We're looking for Dave Jackson," James said.

The guy at the door shook his head. "Dave's not here."

James showed him his badge and said, "Where is he?"

The stoner shrugged. "He went somewhere."

Elizabeth scowled. "We know he went somewhere, genius. We want to know *where* he is right *now*."

This got an eye roll. "He doesn't tell me, dude. We're just roommates. I barely even see him."

"Do you have his phone number?"

"Yeah, I guess."

"Is he, by any chance, out *'urban exploring?'*" She hated using that word. It sounded too glamorous, too cool. Like she was encouraging it.

He nodded. "Think so. That's usually what that freak does on the weekends."

"Okay, I want you to call him up and ask him where he is. And I'd better see some believable acting from you. I don't want him to know who wants to know, if you catch my drift. I need you to pretend you want to join him."

"Dude, he's not going to believe that! I make fun of him all the time."

Now it was Elizabeth's turn to roll her eyes. "Tell him that you have a friend over and that when you told him what your roommate does—like crawling around old, decrepit crap holes—he really wanted to go. And if he tells you where he is, your friend can meet up with him."

"What if he doesn't want company?"

"Oh, I don't know! Tell him your buddy will bring a six-pack."

The guy's eyes narrowed. "What if he knows I'm making it up?"

"Trust me, he doesn't think you're intelligent enough to make stuff up."

They waited while he made the call. They didn't move from the foyer. They knew better. There'd be no point in searching without a warrant. And surely Dave would keep anything incriminating in his own bedroom, which they had no cause to enter. The idiot, to his credit, pulled off the ruse and came back with an address scrawled on a Domino's Pizza coupon. Dave was out exploring an old high school.

The roommate was still on the phone with Dave when he handed over the coupon. Dave had requested Coronas.

Elizabeth pulled the roommate close and whispered, "Ask him how to get into the building."

He quickly had an answer for her. There was a small window at the back of the building adjacent to a blue dumpster.

James wagged a finger at him. "Keep in mind that if you call him back and warn him we are coming, we can charge you with obstruction."

Elizabeth wasn't too worried about him doing that. The guy had already dropped the phone and was staring into space, probably thinking about pizza. She hurried James out of there, wondering how she could put the fear of the Almighty in Dave.

THE NEIGHBORHOOD the school was located in wasn't

the kind of place a normal person would go traipsing about. Fortunately, they already knew Dave wasn't normal. They approached the building stealthily, keeping in mind that these explorer types were attuned to things like approaching cars, always on the lookout for security, if nothing else. So Elizabeth and James parked two blocks away and hoofed it.

They kept their talking to a minimum. It seemed appropriate under the circumstances. The area looked like it had lost its will to keep up with the times forty years ago. It had been abandoned in every sense. Although the whole 'urban exploring' thing bugged her, she wondered if she might be annoyed because she was a little jealous. After all, what did she do with her free time, except watch television or play video games? At least these "explorers" had a quirky kind of companionship, and the thrill of danger had a tendency to create bonds between people. She had some experience with it, too, with her old partner, Chris. After all of the high-pressure stings they'd been a part of, it was probably inevitable that they fell into bed. A year of dangerous situations had felt like a decade of getting to know each other. It was unfortunate it had ended the way it did. That was one lesson she'd never forget.

They found the window Dave had mentioned without any trouble. It was the only one that was open. Most of them had hard metal screens covering the glass. This one had had the screen removed somehow, but it was nowhere to be seen, which probably meant Dave hadn't done it himself, so they couldn't arrest him for that.

When they came upon Dave, he was taking a picture of a classroom. At least a dozen desks were haphazardly stacked on top of each other, looking like any slight disturbance would knock the whole tower over at once. The fluorescent light fixtures in the ceiling were hanging open with their bulbs missing and an entire section of the ceiling had fallen down. It was one of those ceilings Elizabeth remembered well from school, made up of spongy tiles that you could hurl a pencil up into.

Elizabeth walked up behind Dave as he snapped. "Surprise."

Dave whirled around at the sound of her voice. Probably just the fact that it was a woman speaking gave him a shock, and then he saw who had spoken and physically froze up. "I didn't break in. The window was already open."

"Right. I should take your word for it."

"I took pictures coming in. It's a part of my method. Every step along the way, including the entry point. I follow the motto very seriously."

"The motto?"

"'*Take only pictures, leave only footprints.*'"

Elizabeth stepped forward and shoved the printed pictures at him. "What is this?"

He looked at them and frowned. "I'm sorry. I knew those pictures would piss you off, but I took them as an observer. I don't usually happen upon a crime scene. I couldn't pass up the opportunity to document one."

"If you knew they would piss me off, why did you leave them for me?"

"What do you mean? You took my memory card. I didn't *want* you to see them."

James showed Dave the manila envelope. "Did you drop this off at Detective Stratton's house today?"

"No. How would I even know where she lives?"

Elizabeth's head was spinning. It couldn't be. She

couldn't believe that someone at the station would do this to her. Then again, maybe she *could* believe it. One of Chris's old friends, maybe, someone who thought she should have been the one to transfer to Miami Beach.

James looked at her. "Has to be someone on our end. You *did* take his memory card."

"That's right," Dave said. "This isn't what it seems like."

A second guy walked into the room and nearly stumbled over a piece of curled up linoleum when he saw Elizabeth. He was positively staring at her and she felt the hairs on her arms stand on end. Then the guy raised a small Nikon and snapped a picture.

"What are you doing?" James demanded. "She's not a part of the scenery."

"It's *her*," he said. "Did something go down here, too?"

Dave's camera was hanging from his neck. It bumped against his chest as he hurried across the room. "Shut up! Don't you have somewhere else to be?"

The guy held up his hands. "Whoa, chill out. I just thought maybe you found another body. You're a regular Jessica Fletcher, Dave."

Elizabeth moved between the two men, facing Dave. "You somehow have copies of these pictures, don't you?"

"No."

"Then how does this guy know what I look like?"

"He can tell you're detectives just by looking at you. He's must be assuming you're the one I told him about. Obviously I told people about what happened that night."

James scowled and looked at the new guy. "All right,

here's the deal. Get arrested for breaking and entering, or give me the details on Dave. Did he show you any pictures?"

"Yeah."

"Like these?"

He looked at the photos. "Yeah."

Dave was groaning into his hands. "Thanks a lot."

"I'm not getting arrested for you."

James looked at Dave, then back at the guy. "How did he show you the pictures? Were they printed up like this?"

"Yeah."

Dave made another sound of exasperation.

Elizabeth nodded. "So it's back to you. How do you still have those pictures? And if you lie to us one more time…"

"When I was in the closet, I uploaded the pictures from my memory card onto my computer." He shuffled over to the side of the room toward a large camera bag —the same one he'd been carrying two nights ago. He pulled out the second, smaller camera and put it on the floor. Then he reached in deep and pulled out a small netbook and held it up in the air to show them. "I backed it all up on here."

James rolled his eyes. "At least that explains the closet."

"Okay, great," Elizabeth said. "Now I want to know how you found out where I live."

"I don't know where you live. I didn't drop off any pictures for you. That part is the truth. The pictures I showed Ronald didn't look exactly like the ones you're holding. My copies were excellent quality glossies."

"Aside from the police department, you are the only one with these pictures."

"That's not true." He frowned and took a step backward. "I posted them on the Internet."

"You did *what?*"

"It's art! Those are the best pictures I've ever taken. And they mean something. Look at those pictures and tell me they're beautiful. It's a heroic set of images, of Detective Stratton caring about her work—caring deeply. You should be thanking me. This could make you famous."

"Have you even considered the family of our victim? She has people who love her, a mother, maybe a sister, a brother, a husband, a *kid,* for God's sake! They don't want to see her like this. And they sure as hell don't want other people to see her like this. Show some respect."

"Look, I put them on my blog. It's highly unlikely that her family would stumble across them. And I thought you didn't know who she was? Her family probably doesn't even know she's dead."

"You'd better hope they don't find out by reading your blog." Elizabeth thrust her notebook and a pen at him. "Write down the URL for your blog. When I check on it tomorrow, those pictures had better be gone."

On the way back to the car, she stopped on the sidewalk and turned to James. "How likely is it that the killer found those pictures and decided they'd make a great gift for yours truly?"

He frowned and abruptly pulled a can of tobacco from his jacket pocket. "Seems unlikely the killer would know anything about Dave's blog…unless he knows Dave. Or *is* Dave."

CHAPTER 8

Nick kicked off his shoes and made himself comfortable on the couch. “So our killer is leaving Elizabeth presents.”

James had called Nick in the car and he’d arrived at her house at the same time that they did, bearing three lattes and a half-dozen donuts. It was probably the only good thing to happen to her all day.

She sipped the latte. “Maybe we're jumping to conclusions. There's a good chance this has nothing to do with the crimes. These were on the Internet, so there's no telling how many people viewed the images. Anyone who wanted to spook me could have done it.”

Nick put down half of a boston crème donut. “Maybe the killer likes to see you admiring his work. Maybe it turns him on to see a beautiful woman next to the woman he killed.”

Elizabeth blushed and put down the donut she’d been nibbling.

James was nodding at the other end of the couch.

"Who else could it be? It makes more sense that it's someone involved with the case. Like the perpetrator."

"It could be the beekeeper we hired to help us at the hotel. It got pretty heated up there. I don't think he walked away liking me very much. Maybe he wanted to scare me."

"I don't know," Nick said. "How often do you have multiple men furious with you?"

She shook her head sadly. "More than I'd like to admit."

"Well, it had better not be the beekeeper, because I don't know who else we're going to call if this happens again."

"God forbid it happens again," she said quickly, as though his casual comment could make it happen.

"No matter what, it's creepy. We can all agree with that, right?" Nick asked.

Nick nodded and Elizabeth said, "No disagreement here."

"All right, great. So I think we can also agree that Elizabeth shouldn't stay here."

She nearly spit her coffee onto him. "Excuse me?"

"It's not safe."

She shook her head. "He wasn't actually in the house, and I know how to keep myself safe. Last but not least, I have a gun, and I'm not afraid to use it. I'm not a civilian."

James just shook his head. "You can stay at my place."

"And put your daughter at risk? Not a chance."

"A hotel, then."

"Like the Roosevelt?"

"Seriously," James said. "You'd be a lot safer in most hotels. He won't be getting through one of those fire doors. Even if he somehow got a key, you'll have it double bolted from the inside. And every night, Nick and I could make sure he's not in there waiting for you."

"This is Miami. I'm not going to be able to get a room for less than two hundred bucks a night. I can't afford that."

"You can stay with Nick."

Nick shrugged. He'd stayed silent for the entire conversation without indicating whose side he was on.

"No," she said, looking away.

"Just 'no'? You don't have a good reason?"

An image of Chris popped into her head like a warning. "I'd end up committing homicide myself if I had to spend that much time around Nick. No offense."

"None taken," Nick said.

"I understand your concern, but I'll be fine. If you want, you can do the whole SWAT team routine when I come home every night. Then we'll know no one is waiting for me inside. And when I'm asleep, I'll keep my weapon in the room with me. It's not like anyone could get in here without making a lot of noise. I'm a light sleeper."

James was pacing. He stopped in front of Nick. "Aren't you going to talk some sense into her?"

Nick looked up at her from the couch. He looked pretty comfortable. In fact, while she watched, he stretched his legs out on the coffee table and sank a few more inches into the couch cushions. "I could stay here with her."

"Absolutely not," she replied.

"Sorry, James. She isn't going to change her mind." He yawned. "She never does."

James checked his watch. "I need to get home to my

daughter. And my nanny's going to quit if I keep coming home this late."

Nick was still sitting on the couch after James was gone.

Elizabeth busied herself by cleaning up the coffee cups and donut box, hoping he'd have moved by the time she got back. She took longer than she needed to in the kitchen, and when she reentered her living room, he was standing up.

"Thanks for stopping by," she said, moving toward the door.

He came closer, towering over her in her bare feet. "I could spend the night, Elizabeth."

She felt her face heat up. "I'll be okay. Honestly."

Nick watched her, not breaking eye contact, as she was wont to do. "I meant on the couch."

"I *know* that." Now she went all the way to the door and actually opened it up. "Thanks anyway. See you tomorrow?"

"Sure," he said, chuckling to himself as he walked back to his car. "If this gets to be too much, I noticed they're hiring at Dunkin Donuts."

"Screw you," she said and slammed the door.

ALAN CALLED her early in the morning. He'd been up all night analyzing her brand samples. And she'd given him a lot of samples. This deserved more than coffee and donuts, though what, she didn't know. She and James went to the lab first thing.

"I'm sorry, but they didn't match."

Elizabeth stared at him as though he'd change his story if she glared hard enough. "None of them?"

"Nope."

James twirled his coke can behind his back. "Were any of them close?"

"Well...I don't know if that would help you."

"We'll decide that," James said.

He handed him a printout. "That has all the details, but to summarize: the sample from Karina's mouth was closest to the Orange Blossom honey."

"That's made here, isn't it?" she asked.

"Yes, but not exclusively. California is a big producer, as well."

"Was there anything else you could determine?" James asked.

"I think it may have been locally harvested. I don't think you're dealing with some guy who's buying honey for his tea at Publix and then saving it for his extracurricular activities later that day. There are a few signs that this isn't commercial."

"Like what?"

"It seems to be unprocessed." He held the test tube up to the light. It shone golden and translucent, with small particles floating through the goo. "Do you see those little bits floating around? Those are wax particles. You aren't going to find those in Sue Bee Honey bears."

"It looks dirty," Elizabeth said.

"Exactly. Commercial honey has been heat-treated to allow for better consistency and to help prevent crystallization. This shows no sign of that process."

"So this guy probably picked the stuff up at a farmer's market or even on the side of the road." James said. "Or the killer keeps bees and uses the honey he produces."

"When did you last see someone selling honey on the side of the road?" Elizabeth asked him.

"I'm just saying."

Elizabeth took the test tube of honey in her hand. It felt warm, and she could almost imagine a slight vibration coming off of it, as though it were alive. "So is this the end of the road? Would I be wasting my time by bringing more honey—even different brands?"

"Probably. You could check local farmer's markets, as James mentioned, and maybe you'll get lucky, but the quality of this honey is pretty poor."

Elizabeth sighed, shoulders slumping in defeat. She wouldn't be returning to Nick triumphant. She'd be accused of wasting time on a dead end.

"I did call my friend, the botanist," Alan continued. "He's kind of intrigued by what you're doing, and he'd love to meet up." He handed her a small piece of paper. "He said to call him anytime. He's even willing to meet you at the research farm."

"Sounds exciting," James said.

Alan gave him a look. "There's more science to the whole thing than you'd expect. You would learn a lot."

Elizabeth steered James out of there, calling over her shoulder, "Thanks, Alan. Owe you one."

"That's two," he said right before the door clicked closed.

IT WASN'T a great way to start the day, and James said he needed a McDonald's sweet tea to ease his pain. Before they could go, they heard some good news from the CSU department. They had found Karina Brookes on the tapes from the Roosevelt Hotel. She was walking in the lobby with an older man, just as the bartender, Linda, had described. Now all they had to do was find the guy.

And when they arrived at the lab, there was even more evidence to consider.

Michael, the head technician, greeted them and then went straight into telling them what he had found. "I pieced together the glass from the crime scene. We recovered most of it."

"Wow," James said.

The glass was formed into a jar, which had been painstakingly glued together bit by bit. There were some holes missing—inevitably from the pieces the beekeeper had crushed beneath his boots. It was sitting on a light table, making it appear to glow from beneath.

"First thing we did," Michael said, "before we even put it together, was to do some testing on the dirtier pieces. We found traces of honey."

Elizabeth looked at the jar, imagining it filled and golden. "Must have been the container the killer carried the honey in. Like Alan said, the honey isn't commercial."

"Exactly," he said. He pointed to the raised design on the front. "After we got it together, the impression on the glass was discernible. That, along with some small markings on the bottom, led us to the company that manufactured the jar."

"Please tell me it's uncommon."

"It is, but I'm afraid that's not going to help us much. The company went out of business ten years ago. We haven't been able to get any accurate records on distribution or anything else."

Elizabeth wrote down the name of the company. Maybe she could dig something up on her own. "Ten years, huh? So someone either had that jar lying around, or the honey's been packaged for a long time."

James sighed. "Great. So the bottom line is that the Great Honey Search is a cold case."

The technician lost his smile. "Well, it was just a side mission. The results could have proved something more interesting, granted. Don't forget: we have a lot of evidence from the body and the scene. And we're still sorting through garbage."

"We just need a suspect to try and match it to," Elizabeth said. "Have you had a chance to match any of your samples to the group we sent to you? The urban explorers?"

"Not yet. Sorry."

James's phone rang and he stepped away to answer it. He barely spoke into it, then hung up and came back to her side. "A farmer found a hand in an illegal apiary on his land. Nick is there now. We might finally get a name for Jane Doe without having to wait for DNA results."

IT TOOK LESS than twenty-four hours to get a name. Alice English. Nick left to handle the interview with her family. Whether Nick realized it or not, Elizabeth appreciated it greatly. She was trying to hide it as best she could, but she was exhausted. Practically dead on her feet. She had insisted on staying in her home, and she still thought it was the best decision, but she had spent hours tossing and turning, unable to sleep for fear of her home being invaded. The previous night, she could have sworn she heard someone in her backyard. It had sent her leaping out of bed in only a thin camisole and panties to check every window and door. She hadn't found anything amiss, but had still spent the rest of the night with one eye open.

Telling someone their loved one was dead and watching the light drain from their eyes was the worst part of her job. Being tired made her emotionally vulnerable, and liable to lose it during the notification. Not exactly the professional, reassuring impression expected of her.

Nick called them a half-hour later to give them some details. There were two different friends that needed to be tracked down, either of which might know more about Alice on the night she went missing. Apparently, her family hadn't even known she was gone. Nick couldn't do it alone, but Elizabeth already had plans with the forensic botanist. He was meeting her on a research property in Homestead for what he called a "show and tell." So Elizabeth and James split up, James heading for South Beach to interview one of Alice's friends, and Elizabeth heading for Homestead.

It was a long, boring drive.

The research facility made her think of the old manor houses, where the rest of the neighborhood was filled with the small abodes of the tenants looking up at the cold, lonely estate. It had darkened windows, like a neglected summer cottage, and huge oak trees that concealed most of the building from the street.

The day was hot, and she groaned when she stepped out of the car and into the humid August air. The sky was as black as it had been the entire week, giving the weathermen on the local news stations hard-ons in anticipation of the next big meteorological event. They had been saying that a tropical depression was about to hit, and they were right, to a degree: it *was* depressing.

As instructed, she avoided the front door and walked around the side of the home. She peeked in the windows as she did so, and thought she could see white sheet-covered furniture through the dusty panes.

Behind the building, she saw a man crouching next to one of the largest trees, searching through a large, metal box. He was humming quietly to himself, a tune that carried on the wind. "Hello!" she called out.

He jumped and dropped something that looked like a pair of blunt scissors back into the box. "Oh, hello there. You must be the detective."

"Guilty." She adjusted the sunglasses that were propped up on her head, feeling stupid for even having them on her person. "Patrick Mulrohney?"

"Last time I checked."

"Thank you so much for meeting with me on such short notice."

"Don't even mention it. This is exactly the kind of stuff that interests me. You're doing me a favor." Mulrohney gestured to the yard sloping down from the house. It was a large collection of apiary boxes, lined up in neat little rows. "We can talk while I check on my bees."

She followed him to a small shed that contained all of his supplies.

"Put this on over your clothes." He handed her a beekeeper's suit.

She examined it. "It doesn't seem to offer much more protection than what I'm wearing."

"Well, it has to be a thin material, especially in Florida. If they made it out of Kevlar, you'd melt before you got stung. The suit helps a lot, because it's loose enough that when a bee stings you, their stinger is kept away from the skin." He pulled out the wrist of the suit he was wearing, then snapped it back into place. "You also have elastic cuffs and tight velcro fasteners so the bees can't gain access to the inside of the suit."

"Is the white important?"

"It's a neutral color. Bees are attracted to darker shades." He handed her a hood. "You aren't allergic, are you?"

"Apparently not. I've been stung more times than I'd like recently."

After she'd suited up, Mulrohney put on long leather gloves and retrieved a smoker from the shed. He led the way back to the bee yard.

Elizabeth tried not to feel too intimidated. "You know, before I started this case, I had no idea so many people kept bees."

He opened the top of the smoker and inserted a long-necked lighter. "You'd be surprised. You could be living next door to an amateur beekeeper and never even know it. Florida is one of the top honey-producing states."

"It's funny. I've never liked honey much. Now I like it even less."

He recoiled as if she'd insulted him. "There is much more to an apiary than producing honey. There's propolis, royal jelly, beeswax—all useful in different ways. And still, all those things are just bonuses. Bees pollinate one third of the things that make up the world's diet. We need bees more than they need us."

The smoker was really pumping now, filling the air and blurring her vision. "The beekeeper we brought to the hotel used one of those, as well. How does it work?"

"Two ways: it masks the alarm pheromones that the guard bees would normally release when the hive is disturbed; it also tricks them into believing there is a fire, whereupon they gorge themselves on honey, just in case they are forced to abandon the hive."

"Do you ever get stung in spite of that?"

"All the time."

That wasn't comforting. Even so, she followed him into the field of boxes. He stopped in front of one particular hive and opened it up.

Patrick started shaking his head. "Yep, these guys are on their way out."

Though she was apprehensive, Elizabeth approached and looked inside. The hive was practically empty. The frame Mulrohney was lifting into the air looked spotty and incomplete. The few bees that were clinging to the interior of the box looked slow and weak. "Are they like that because of the smoker?"

"No. This colony is dying."

"Can you save it?"

"No. I'm quite powerless, actually. This is a prime example of a colony collapse, something that makes beekeepers all over the world tear out their hair in big clumps."

"It happens a lot?"

He put the lid back on the hive box. "Unfortunately, it's an epidemic."

"What causes it?"

"There are many theories, but nobody knows for sure. The latest study blames one of the more common pesticides used in the US. Anyway, let's move on. That's not something you have to worry about." He replaced the comb in the box and moved to the next hive.

"So did Alan tell you about the tests he did?"

"You brought him a sample of honey, the base sample. Then he compared the base to a collection of different honeys you collected from around the city."

She nodded. "Unfortunately, none of them matched. Alan believes it's not from any major manufacturer. That it hasn't been processed."

“May I see it?"

She pulled the container out of her pocket.

Mulrohney held it up to the sun. "Definitely unprocessed. Your killer didn't just go into a store and buy honey—he harvested it."

"Or he could have purchased from a local beekeeper."

"That's true. What do you think?"

"I have a feeling that the honey is meaningful to him and, if so, he probably found it on his own. My big question is whether he has his own apiary, or if he's stealing it."

Mulrohney was pulling the frames from each box and checking them. “The honey isn't ready to be collected until all the combs are capped off with wax.”

It did appear incomplete. "So Alan said you could help me in a way he couldn't."

He nodded. "It's my research. I'm being paid the big bucks to work on pollination source tracking."

"Which is?"

"Analyzing a particular batch of honey to determine what country it came from, what region, and so on. It's all in the particular plant markers." He gestured around him. "In the same way that bees that pollinate orange blossoms make orange blossom honey, every hive has its own particular combination of plants. So I can look at a sample and pick out which plants those bees pollinated when they were making their honey. And, with that information, I can tell you what region they were located in."

"Wouldn't that be random? Different from one harvest to the next?"

"No. Bees are not only creatures of habit, but they always pollinate in a three-mile radius of their hive. Since we know that, we can be very specific when we compare a honey's plant content to charts of local flora."

"I had no idea. I mean, I'd seen clover honey before, but I didn't really put much thought into it." Then she connected the dots and realized what he was saying. "So you're telling me you can analyze this honey and tell me which apiary the killer got the honey from?"

"I hope so. Of course, you might have a problem if there are too many apiaries in one area. Like if my neighbor on each side also had them, it would be harder to distinguish one from the other. Fortunately—or unfortunately, depending on who you ask—we backyard beekeeper are usually more spread out than that. I might be able to get you very close."

"That's amazing. That could solve the case."

Mulrohney smiled like a toddler who'd just been told he was a good boy.

THE REST of the week went by without any new developments.

"You have an interesting look on your face," James said, taking a large bite of a New York-style slice of pizza with oil bubbling on its surface.

"I was just thinking about my soda. This is *really* good Diet Coke."

"There's a difference?"

She nodded, looking around the hole-in-the-wall

pizza joint they were sitting in. "At some places, they don't put enough of the syrup in the machine, so it tastes like soda water. Here, they keep it really sweet. What can I say? I appreciate the simple things in life."

"Damn straight." James looked toward the plate glass window of Steve's Pizza, then his head whipped back to her. "Don't look now—it's McQuinn."

Of course she looked. It was human nature. Past the row of pepper plants decorating decades-old green formica booths, Captain McQuinn was walking through the door next to the Ms. Pacman machine. He'd come with Franklin. Elizabeth quickly looked away. "I don't want to talk to him right now."

"Think of it this way: he's already read the latest report. He can't be expecting anything different to come out of our mouths." James ripped a sheet of paper towel off the roll from a wooden stand on the table and blotted his hands. "You think someone else could have worked this case better? I don't."

"I don't either."

"There you go." He lowered his voice. The captain was ordering at the register, seemingly fn bga.,gm˜/ oblivious. "It's not our fault this isn't one of the easier ones to solve. And we will solve it. It's only been ten days. And Nick hasn't mentioned any issues."

Elizabeth was facing the side of the restaurant where the register was located, surreptitiously watching McQuinn in her peripheral vision. She saw him pay for the order, step out of line, and turn in her direction. She made a big effort not to show any disappointment.

"Taking a break?"

"Did you find a booth?" she asked. "You'd better grab

one. You know how quickly they get snapped up at this time of day."

He nodded. "Franklin's taking care of it."

She saw Franklin sit in the booth diagonal from theirs. He looked up and smiled.

The captain looked at the side of the booth James was on. "Do you mind?"

"Of course not."

"Just until my slice is ready," he said, then leaned back casually, as though it were a social call. Then he said, "I read the report."

"What did you think?"

He pursed his lips and looked up. "Not the best."

Elizabeth remembered what James had said and it gave her strength. She glanced at him before saying, "I think we've done really well with what we've been given. We haven't caught any breaks on this one."

"Well, we can't always hope for breaks, Elizabeth."

She smiled nervously. "I know that. I just meant that we've done everything we were supposed to do. Unfortunately, it hasn't panned out yet. We do have a good lead with the guy at the bar, though."

"Yeah, I wanted to talk to you about that."

James put down his cup of Coke. "He looks really good for it. Karina didn't have any enemies, and she wasn't involved in anything fishy. So it's looking like a date gone bad. A lot of people saw Karina leave the bar with this guy. The only goal now is to pinpoint who he is."

McQuinn nodded with a skeptical look on his face. "The guy should already be in our custody."

Elizabeth blinked, her contacts suddenly feeling dry and a sick feeling bubbling in the pit of her stomach. "How so?"

"On Thursday, the bartender at Normandy's—I believe her name is Linda—tried to call, but couldn't get in touch with either of you."

Elizabeth felt as if the bottom had fallen out of her stomach, like an elevator she was riding in had just plunged to the basement. Tower of Terror, all right. She started shaking her head. "I don't understand. Why wouldn't Linda be able to get in touch with us? She has both of our cards, and we're always available." Elizabeth started debating it in her head. Had Linda called in the middle of the night? Elizabeth slept with the phone on her bedside table, but it was possible she had slept through the ringing. She thought she'd made sure it was loud enough to hear over the sound of her IPod, but maybe it wasn't. Maybe she'd screwed up.

"You know how important it is for a detective to always be available."

"I *am* always available." She touched her Blackberry as if to reassure herself it was still there. That it hadn't disappeared, stolen by the evil detective-undermining fairies.

"It was my fault," James said, his accent suddenly seeming stronger. "I forgot my phone on my desk on Thursday. I'm sorry. I guess I really screwed up this time."

McQuinn glanced at him, then back at Elizabeth. "Exactly."

The pizza-tossing guy called out the captain's name, but Franklin went to pick it up from the counter. McQuinn didn't budge. Franklin gave her a consoling look as he walked by. Her gaze flowed from him to another detective sitting in the booth directly behind James. He looked away guiltily.

The captain tapped the pock-mocked wood table.

"So, as you can see, a huge mistake has already been made in this investigation. Linda kept him there as long as she could, but it was all for nothing. Who knows if she'll even bother calling the next time he comes in?"

"Is it really necessary to do this in public?"

"What difference does it make? Nobody is paying attention. The world doesn't revolve around you, as much as you might think it does."

That was usually a pretty good line to put someone in their place, except that she couldn't imagine it being less true. No, the world didn't revolve around her, but she got way more than her fair share of attention in the department. For one thing, female homicide detectives were still in the minority. Then there was her reputation as being trigger-happy, and now being assigned a high profile case. If the captain didn't think people were paying attention to her every move, he was fooling himself. She sat in silence, realizing she couldn't say any of this without sounding petty and immature. All she would get is a condescending laugh and some comment to indicate that she was "so young." She knew the drill. "No, I suppose it doesn't, sir, although I think doing this back at the station would have been more professional. I'm sure you already considered that and dismissed it for a good reason."

"Let's get down to brass tacks," James said. "Are you saying we're off the case?"

"No, no, don't get hasty. I'm going to give you both another chance. Or, I guess I should say a *third* chance in your case, Elizabeth."

She inhaled sharply and blinked some more. It seemed that at times like this, her body sucked all the moisture out of her eyes. Which made her eyes start to water in response. Which could be mistaken for tears.

And she sure as hell wasn't going to cry in front of this asshole. James must have seen all of this in her expression, as he calmly said, "Thank you, sir. We really appreciate that."

Elizabeth could smell the crushed red peppers that the guy behind her was sprinkling on his pizza, as well as the cloud of garlic powder fogging the air. She stared at the Bud Light sign above the pickup counter, the one that had long since stopped flashing, then looked back at McQuinn.

He'd been waiting for her to speak. Waiting for the blowup.

Her voice was very calm when she finally spoke. "So how do you know Linda called us?"

"She contacted me when she couldn't find either of you." He stood up. "You're going to keep putting all your effort into this case, correct? You won't let me down?"

"I won't sleep until it's solved."

"Good." He walked to the booth he was sharing with Franklin and sat with his back to Elizabeth. Conversation over. Sayonara, Stratton.

"Wow," James said quietly. "I'm so sorry, Elizabeth. I ran back for my phone so quickly. It had to have been less than thirty minutes. And I didn't have any messages. Wouldn't she have left a voicemail or something?"

"You'd think so, wouldn't you?" She shook her head. "I don't blame you. It's just a bad coincidence. What's more, Linda couldn't have called me. I don't know if the captain got bad information or made some wrong assumptions, but I would have answered my phone."

"Weird. All right, onwards and upwards. We're not going to let this weigh us down. He'll go back to that bar, and we'll get him. *If* he's our killer, which he probably isn't."

"I guess you're right," she said. They both fell silent. She picked up her second slice of pizza three times, but each time felt too nauseated to eat it. She gave up and took a sip of Diet Coke. It tasted like soda water.

CHAPTER 9

They spent the rest of the day filling out paperwork in companionable silence. A mind-numbing, but necessary, task. When it got late, they walked to the parking garage together.

As Elizabeth was getting in her car, James said, "Get some rest. I know you were thrown for a loop today, and I'm sorry for my part in it."

"I don't blame you."

"Just promise me you'll do something to take your mind off of it. Your job can't be your entire world."

As she drove home, she kept repeating the conversation with the captain in her head, coming up with better responses to his accusations and some pretty good comebacks. They at least made her smile, even though she'd never use them.

She thought about Linda. She couldn't get what had happened out of her head, especially the part where she had supposedly missed a phone call. Maybe the captain didn't realize it, but she was meticulous about her phone. It was always on, always charged, and always clipped to her belt. It was gun on the right and Blackberry on the left. She even slept with it.

She drove right past the exit that would have taken her home and continued on I-95 until it turned into US-1, almost on autopilot. She never actually decided to go to the Roosevelt—her body was doing it for her.

Linda was laughing with a bald-headed man at the end of the bar, twirling a cherry on its stem. She saw Elizabeth approach and straightened up to move away from the guy. "What happened the other night? That guy was in here, sitting right over there like nothing had ever happened."

"I don't know. I was hoping you could help me with that."

"I waited, but you never showed up." She started to wipe down the bar with the towel that she'd picked up from behind her. "Did you not get the message?"

Elizabeth shook her head. Now she was really confused. "Okay, let's start from the beginning. I never received a call from you. I was told that you tried to call both James and me, but never got through."

"Who told you that?" She had stopped wiping now, her towel frozen in place.

"Someone in the department. It doesn't matter. I actually came here to find out whom you'd spoken to because someone would have had to have known you called. Is this making any sense?"

"They're raking you over the coals, aren't they?"

"I'm afraid so. They know all about the guy being here and apparently I missed my opportunity. So what's the real deal?"

She shook her head. "I didn't call you, I called James."

"And you left a voicemail?"

Linda handed one of her regulars a Michelob Ultra,

then turned back to Elizabeth. "I don't know what's going on over on your end, but I called the number on James's card. I knew it wasn't him as soon as he answered, but he said he could take a message."

"Did he say who he was?"

"No, but he took what I said very seriously. He said you guys would be down here in five minutes, but you never came."

Elizabeth was feeling disgusted, even a bit nauseated.

"And then," Linda continued, "Well, I thought this was odd, but I thought maybe I was being paranoid. The more I think about it though..."

"What?"

"Well, soon after the guy left, someone I'd never seen before came to the bar. Well, of course, that happens all the time. This isn't Cheers. This guy had that look about him though, that swagger. You don't have it so much, but it's something all the cops have that makes it easy to spot them."

"You think it was a cop."

"Yep. He was dressed down, too, not in a suit or anything. I don't know...anyway, I thought I might have been right about it because he didn't order anything and left after only five minutes."

"I don't suppose you see much of that kind of behavior."

"Nope." Linda paused to greet a man who had joined her behind the bar. "None of this even matters though."

Elizabeth tried to guess as to what she was talking about and failed. "Why is that?"

Linda turned to the side, looking at a guy down the bar. "Apparently, Max has a confession to make."

Elizabeth followed her gaze and realized Linda was

looking at the regular they'd spoken to on their first visit to the bar. She stood up and approached him this time. Linda followed behind the bar.

Max looked a lot more uncomfortable than he had the first time she'd spoken to him.

"Linda tells me you have something to share."

He frowned. "That guy you're looking for, I know him. His name is George Hamish. He's my father."

Elizabeth's pulse surged. "Why didn't you tell me that before?"

"I was hoping you'd find out some other way. He and I don't exactly have a good relationship. I was humiliated when he followed me here that night. Tried to pick up some girl half his age."

"So I guess you have a good idea where we can find him."

"Yeah, but I honestly don't think he killed anyone."

"We're not saying he did," Elizabeth said, leaning casually on the bar with her elbows. "He was the last person seen with the victim. It's very important that we speak with him."

He accepted the notebook and pen she handed him and started writing. "He works at a twenty-four hour urgent care clinic. He'll be there now."

"Thank you, Max. You've been very helpful." She turned to Linda. "And thank you, Linda. Once again, you're a life saver."

"How about I walk you out? I get to go home early tonight. Wanted to be awake for my son's birthday tomorrow. Are you going to talk to that guy now?"

"Yes. I have to get my partner first. He's going to love this. He's probably fast asleep."

They'd reached Linda's Honda Civic and she

unlocked the doors with a wireless key fob. "Tell your partner I say hi, will you?"

"Of course," Elizabeth said, then walked away with her phone in hand, hoping James would focus more on the fact that they'd finally found the guy than on the lateness of the hour.

~

THE CLINIC WAS in North Miami. They parked easily in the back and walked into a small waiting area that had the typical blue speckled fabric chairs, low end tables with a variety of magazines, and a clouded window on the opposite wall. A woman in the corner was coughing into a surgical mask beneath a sign advising that no cell phones were allowed, but other than that, the place was empty. James was about to knock on the glass when it slid open.

"Hi, can I help you?" the receptionist asked in a tone that was both welcoming and concerned.

"We're the detectives who called a half-hour ago. Is George Hamish available?"

"Oh, yes, of course. Why don't you come through the door on your far right? He can speak to you in his office."

Elizabeth squirted some hand sanitizer onto her hands from the dispenser on the counter and then followed James into the back.

A man met them in the hallway. "Sandra said you wanted to speak to me?"

"Yes," James said, gesturing away from the reception area. "Can we go—"

"Sure. It's just down here." Hamish walked ahead of them, not showing any signs of concern. His age seemed to be about mid- to late-forties, just as Linda had estimated, but he wore it rather well. He had a full head of dark brown hair that showed only the slightest trace of gel. He was dressed in gray slacks and a light blue checked shirt. He wouldn't pass for a man in his twenties, but he certainly looked healthy, and more than capable of choking the life out of a young woman.

"What do you do here so late?" James asked after he nonchalantly placed his card on the desk and sat in one of the visitors' chairs.

Hamish sat behind his desk. It made Elizabeth and James look like customers and it was just another day at work. "Billing, general managerial duties. I actually spend most of my time out front with Sandra. We like to have two people at reception whenever possible."

"Do you always work the night shift?"

"Me and another guy take turns. There's a lot of stuff I need to do in the daytime, as well." He picked up a loose pencil on his desk and dropped it into a plain mug.

Elizabeth didn't see any personal pictures. No frames with family photos from Disney World. "Are you married, George?"

"I'm a widower."

"I'm sorry to hear that. Children?"

"Two." Hamish leaned back in his chair, making it creak loudly against the strain. "I'm sorry, but what is this about?"

"We're here to ask you some questions about Karina Brookes," James said.

"Who?"

"Were you at the Roosevelt Hotel bar two weeks ago Friday?"

"Roosevelt Hotel bar," he repeated slowly. "Yes, I believe I was. That's the place in the Gables?"

"Did you meet a woman named Karina Brookes?" James asked. He was excellent at playing it cool. Elizabeth bet if she were a suspect, she wouldn't realize she was in trouble.

He glanced away, his eyes glazing over. "I met a woman that night, yes, but to be honest with you, I can't be positive about her name."

Elizabeth pulled the notebook out of her jacket pocket. She showed him a picture of Karina.

"Yes, I met that woman." He seemed proud, as though he were happy he could agree with them. "So what happened? Did she say I did something to her?"

James shrugged. "Why would you assume that's what we're here for?"

The guy laughed sheepishly. "Come on, I'm not stupid. Two detectives come to speak to me about a drunk woman I met one night in a bar. That's really the only thing that makes sense."

"Well, if you don't mind answering a few more questions, we'll get to why we're here."

"Oh, sure. Go ahead."

"What happened when you left the bar with Karina?"

"Not that much, unfortunately. Like I said, she was kind of drunk, so we ended up kissing in the stairwell." He looked at Elizabeth, then down at his desk. "After a little bit of that, she pulled away and started yelling at me. She said that I was disrespecting her and that she wasn't a whore."

"Then what happened?" asked James.

"I left. She obviously wasn't interested, and I wasn't

going to stick around. I mean, this sort of thing is what I was afraid of if I did stay with her. I realized she might be drunker than I thought. So even if I could have somehow sweet-talked her into sleeping with me, she might call it rape when she woke up in the morning. No thank you."

Elizabeth made a couple notes, then looked up and asked, "How did you leave the hotel? What exit did you take?"

"I don't know. It was a door that led to the back alley. When I was in the stairwell, I saw the exit sign and decided to go that way instead of the way I had come in. She was acting a little crazy, so I didn't want to go back into the lobby and have her follow me screaming."

"Convenient," James said to Elizabeth and she nodded.

"Now do I get to know what's going on?"

James laced his fingers together and leaned forward. "Karina Brookes was found dead on an empty floor of the hotel just a couple of floors above where you claim to have seen her last."

"What?" Hamish looked a lot more shocked than she would have expected of him. His gaze started to shift around the room, bouncing from one object to the next, while his mouth remained slightly agape. "She's dead? Someone killed her?"

"I'm afraid so."

"How did they kill her?"

"He—*or she,* I suppose—strangled her." James just kept his eyes on Hamish, his gaze never wavering.

"And you're here because you think I might have done it?" He appeared incredulous.

James simply nodded. "Both security footage and

eyewitness accounts tell the same story. You were the last person seen with her."

He was shaking his head and looking down at his lap. "Was she raped?"

Elizabeth studied his expression carefully, looking for signs of either pride or perverted interest, but she found neither. "Yes. Why do you ask?"

"Because I know for a fact that it wasn't me, and you can prove that sort of stuff with science, can't you? And I also went to work right after I left the hotel. I knew Sandra would be alone here that night, because Raoul called in sick. So I figured I might as well give her a hand instead of going home and feeling sorry for myself."

Elizabeth shared a glance with James. Everything had been looking up, pointing to George Hamish as the killer—at least Karina's killer.

"Can you prove you were here?" she asked.

He nodded. "Sandra can vouch for me, but there's also my timecard. It will show the time I clocked in."

"We'll need to see it," James said.

They were there for another five minutes, shadowing Hamish as he pulled up the timecard and showed them the right entries. He had definitely been working there that night. Then they spoke to Sandra and she also confirmed that he had been there.

"Dead end," Elizabeth said when they were back in the car. "And now we're nowhere. We have no idea who killed Karina, and we can't even pinpoint when Alice died."

James frowned. "Well, at least we're in the right neighborhood to grab a slice. It's on the way home."

"I need something stronger than pizza to fix this disaster."

ELIZABETH CLOSED her front door and stepped into her living room. It was good to be home. She kicked off her shoes, sighing with relief when her bare feet hit the carpet. The place still smelled like the cinnamon candle she'd burned two days ago.

She shuffled into her bedroom, undressing as she walked and letting things fall where they may. The bed beckoned her with its comforter in shades of pale blue and white. There were big fluffy pillows and smaller decorative ones. And though she was just about to throw them all onto the floor, they still made her feel like she was staying in a hotel. A nice one, not the Roosevelt.

She removed the last of her clothing and dropped it next to the nightstand. In the drawer beneath, she found a silky microfiber camisole and comfortable hip-hugging panties to wear. Though she wasn't one to sleep naked, she could never wear much more than that.

After pulling down the comforter on one corner, she sat on the edge of the bed, then slipped her feet between the sheets. *Ah, relief.* She felt a little hazy from the lack of sleep, and was falling into the same routine she had had every night since the photographs had been slipped under her door.

Resting her head on a large white pillow, she stretched out on the cool, crisp sheets. She extended her legs towards the foot of the bed. She froze suddenly as her foot touched something wet. And sticky.

She jerked her foot back and shivered violently. *God, what was that?*

Heart beating rapidly in her chest, she pulled her

feet up. Her whole body was shaking as she fumbled with the bedside lamp. Her hand was clumsy as she felt for the pull string in the dark. Then she found it and yanked hard.

She looked in each dimly lit corner of her bedroom. Then, with dread, she pulled down the bed covers to see what she'd unknowingly dipped her feet into. It was all over the bottom third of her sheets: a thick, golden goo. She leaned forward and smelled it. *Oh my God.*

It was honey.

Her foot was still dripping with the stuff as she leapt onto the carpet. She backed up until she had a view of both windows and the door to the living room. Someone had been in her house. Someone could *still* be in her house.

She grabbed her service pistol from the bedside table and immediately took off the safety. She stood there, alone with her thoughts—and they were not good company.

Her robe was hanging on a hook on the back of her bathroom door. She moved in that direction, stopping short when she saw that the door was closed. Had it been closed when she'd left the house that morning?

Once again, she checked all the windows while watching the bathroom door out of the corner of her eye. It was very quiet in the house, and it suddenly seemed painfully so. Her senses were all finely tuned; she was hearing noises that probably occurred all the time, but suddenly seemed loud and ominous. The bathroom in particular seemed to hum like...like a thousand bees.

She stared at the plain wooden door as though staring hard enough would render it transparent. Her cell phone was still next to her bed and she picked it up and dialed Nick, praying he would pick up. She didn't want to have to call James—not when he had his daughter at home. And Nick's house was much closer. As soon as she heard Nick's familiar voice, she blurted, "I need you. *Now.*"

"I'll be right there."

"Get here as soon as you can!" She hung up and blinked back tears.

Sweat was beading on her upper lip as she slowly approached the bathroom. She'd gone through extensive training on how to approach situations like this. It wasn't the time to wimp out. Exhaling a long, painful breath, she realized it was time to find her voice.

"I have a loaded weapon pointed at the door and I will be coming in. I suggest you come out now with your hands above your head. I'll give you to the count of five, and then I'm coming in. One."

She cocked the gun and made sure her grip was perfect for a one-handed shot. Her hand was shaking even as she gazed down at it, and she made a concentrated effort to stop trembling. *You can do this.*

"Two." Another step closer to the bathroom, and another year shaved off her life.

Every hair on her arms stood up. She heard something. Probably from the bathroom, but she couldn't be sure. She tossed a quick glance over her shoulder before focusing on the door again. "Three," she said, the sound of her own voice echoing painfully through her head.

Why did he have to invade her personal space? Whatever she'd had to deal with in the course of her job, it had never followed her home. This was *her* house. She froze again at the sound of a new noise, until she realized it was her own labored breath.

"Elizabeth." The voice tickled her ears in a sibilant hiss from close behind her.

She whirled around with her gun pointing out, face screwed up in an expression of fear. The moment she saw him, she was almost as afraid as she'd started out—because she felt like she was still about to press down on that trigger. Very carefully, she let the pistol go limp in her hand.

Nick came forward, his own gun at the ready. "Is there someone in the bathroom?"

She quickly turned around and pressed the side of her body against his. "I don't know. I don't remember shutting the door this morning. I just..."

"It's okay. I'm sure it's nothing."

"There was honey. In my bed."

He looked at the bed, then back at the bathroom door. "How often is that door shut? You know, in your normal daily routine."

"Maybe once every couple of weeks. Why would I shut it? I'm always alone."

He nodded. "Why don't you go back into the living room? I'll tell you when it's all clear."

"No, we're doing this together." She wiped her damp forehead with the back of her hand and lowered her voice. "You open the door, and I'll cover you from over here. I'll have a good angle on the room. Just remember to duck if someone comes charging out."

"Fat chance of that." He got into position. He put his hand on the doorknob.

She nodded.

Nick threw open the door, then jumped back and gave the room a quick visual sweep with his gun extended.

Elizabeth stood behind him, looking into each

corner that he might have missed, then focused on the shower curtain. It was pulled tight. "Great," she muttered angrily.

With his free hand, Nick pulled a small, round candle out of the decorative wooden boat on her dresser and unceremoniously lobbed it over the metal curtain rod. It made a loud crash in the bottom of the tub. He quickly hurled two more in random directions and they both hit the bottom without any impediment. Finally, he threw one straight at the curtain with an extra jolt of force. Nothing.

He shrugged as if to say, *here goes nothing,* and charged in. He whipped the curtain out of the way, gun at the ready. Then he turned around, putting his back to the tub. "Looks like we're all clear in here."

Her shoulders relaxed for a moment, but then they seemed to realize that the rest of the house also needed to be checked. She and Nick walked through the small house slowly, doing a similar routine as they had done for the bathroom, checking every closet, cupboard, and cabinet. Elizabeth's heart rate never dropped, not until every last room and potential hiding place had been checked.

"This is not okay," she said, backing up. "Why was he in my house? What purpose could it have possibly served?"

"He obviously wants you intimidated. Catching him is your number one priority, and he knows it." He frowned. "Listen, I know a guy at ADT. He'll put you on the shortlist."

She looked at her bed. It was still mostly put together, with the jumbo marshmallow pillows and voluminous down blanket. But it no longer beckoned to her like a safe, enclosed cubbyhole. She'd been ripped from the womb too soon. Then she looked at Nick.

"Wait a second," she said. "What are you wearing?"

She had calmed down enough to look at him, and she couldn't help but stare. He was wearing a thin, sleeveless undershirt. It fit him snugly, showing off a muscular chest and tight abs. But it was his arms that really got her attention. They were large and muscular, perfect for his six foot four frame. He was also wearing dark gray sweatpants, tied low on his hips with a thick drawstring. They seemed in danger of falling down, which made her wonder if he was wearing anything underneath.

Damn, she'd had no idea of what had been hidden beneath those Hugo Boss suits.

She suddenly realized she'd never seen him out of his work clothes before. Clearly, they didn't have a close relationship. She supposed that was mostly her fault. There had been occasions when someone in the department had had a barbeque or a birthday party, but she had never attended any of them.

"Never mind what *I'm* wearing," he replied. "Look at *you*."

Elizabeth almost died on the spot. She'd been too scared to worry about her lack of clothing. She hurried past him into the bathroom and found her robe. He wasn't showing off anything she couldn't see at the gym, but her outfit was way too revealing for Nick to see.

He was still standing in her bedroom when she came out and she got a good look at him from head to foot. He wasn't wearing any shoes. He watched her come to that realization, then matter-of-factly said, "I was across the street."

"What? Where?"

"I'll show you." In a moment, Nick was taking her across the street, through the drizzling rain. He was barefoot. He walked her right into the house across from hers, without using a key.

The house was empty but well kept, with clean, shining tile and soft carpet in the bedrooms. In one of the bedrooms—the one at the front of the house with a window facing the street—there was a sleeping bag, a book, and a pair of binoculars. "You've been staying here?"

"Since you received the photos."

"Why?"

"I didn't think you were safe. Clearly, I was right." He walked across the room and leaned against the front wall. "It's not a big deal. I would just take a look every once in a while and do a couple of nightly walks around the property to make sure nothing was amiss."

Her mouth fell open. "That was you I heard a few nights ago! I thought I heard something in my backyard."

"Yeah, sorry about that." He grinned sheepishly. "That was sloppy. I did enjoy seeing you peer out the window in your underwear."

"You saw that?" She pulled her robe tighter, fiddling with the silky belt.

He grinned. "I'm sorry."

She looked around the room again. In one of the corners there were a couple of extra pillows and a fleece blanket, but they looked untouched. She sighed. "When have you been sleeping?"

He shrugged. "I take a few power naps during the day. Half an hour here, fifteen minutes there…I get by."

"I can't believe you'd do this," she finally said,

shaking her head. "I didn't even think you were concerned. When James was trying to convince me that night, you were very quiet."

"I know you better than James does."

Her face felt hot.

"I knew you wouldn't agree to leaving or to anyone staying with you," he said. "So I figured I'd watch out for you on my own, regardless of what you said. I do care, Elizabeth."

She looked at him standing there, talking about protecting her, with arms on display that were clearly well-equipped to do it. She shivered, finding it difficult to look away.

He was still carrying both guns, and she watched him carefully place them on the carpet next to the sleeping bag. "I'm sure you don't want to sleep in your house tonight. Besides the security risk, you don't have a bed."

"I don't have one here, either," she said.

"True. I can go get some stuff for you, if you like. Clothing, maybe a pillow or two, a sleeping bag, if you have one."

She shook her head and moved closer to him, where it felt safer. "Having never had even the slightest desire to go camping or to a sleepover, I've led a sleeping bag-free life. I guess clothing would be good. Or I could get it in the morning. All I need now is maybe that blanket over there and one of the pillows."

"You can have the sleeping bag, too."

Her eyelids were feeling droopier by the second, so she grabbed the extra bedding, brought it close to the sleeping bag, and laid it out. She kneeled on top of the blanket. "I'm not going to take it. You need to sleep, too."

"I doubt I will tonight," he said, lowering himself to the sleeping bag next to her. "I'd rather keep an eye on things."

God, he even smelled good, she realized now that he was closer to her. Like soap and sweat and gun oil. She couldn't stop looking at his arms and thinking of them wrapped around her. A pleasurable tingle traveled down her legs. "Just lie here with me for a little bit," she said, and couldn't believe she said it. She didn't want to take it back.

He looked a little surprised, too. Then he stretched out on the sleeping bag, raising up his arms and tucking his hands behind his head.

She lowered herself beside him. She could hear him breathing. It sounded deep and steadily reassuring. Then she turned to look at him.

He was looking at her. "Dammit, Elizabeth," he said and rolled over until he was pinning her to the blanket. "Why are you looking at me like that?"

Now her senses were full of him. The masculine smell of him, the tickly stubble of his beard, and his heavy weight on top of her body. "Because I've never seen you like this before, and it's turning me on."

Without a word, he reached down to her waist and untied the belt of her robe. He let it fall open, then looked down at her. "You are one sexy woman."

To answer that, she hooked one of her legs around his hip and pulled him tightly against her. She felt all of him, and knew he wasn't lying.

He pushed against her through the thin pair of pants and groaned. He kissed her long and hard. And he kept kissing her until she was breathless and he was straining against his clothing.

Moments later, his pants were off and her panties

were a damp wad on the carpet. “Oh, God, Nick,” she gasped as he plunged inside her. She tightened both legs around his body, pulling him deeper. “You're so—”

He cut her off with his mouth, kissing her hard again as she writhed beneath him. He kissed down the side of her face, breathing heavily in her ear. His arms were as strong as they looked, and he reached under her body to pull her against him.

She never wanted it to end.

So, as it turned out, neither of them slept much that night.

CHAPTER 10

"Nick, meet Patrick Mulrohney, our official department bee expert."

"Charmed, I'm sure."

Mulrohney picked up an electric kettle and filled it with water from the sink. He was hosting them in the bright, friendly kitchen of his house. "My results are interesting, to say the least."

Elizabeth sat in one of the farmhouse chairs. "Are they going to help us?"

"I think there's a very good chance of that, thanks to the unique markers I found."

James hadn't been present for the first visit, but Elizabeth had explained everything to him. He watched Mulrohney with unconcealed interest, spinning a can of chewing tobacco in his pocket. "We might be able to find the apiary the honey came from? You found an uncommon plant pollen mixed up in there?"

Mulrohney nodded and set the kettle on its base and switched it on. "How about rhododendrons?"

Elizabeth shook her head. "I'm not so familiar with plants."

“Aren't those poisonous?” James asked.

"Yes, they are. Rhododendrons are in the mountain laurel family. They aren’t very common in Florida."

"Does that affect the honey? Make it unsafe to eat?" she asked.

He placed three mugs on the table, then a jar of honey, a crystal bowl of sugar cubes, and a small pitcher of milk. "Yes, it has similarities to *digitalis*—Deadly Nightshade. It could possibly kill you in sufficient doses. That's not—from what I understand—what happened here, right?"

"No, the honey ritual was entirely postmortem,” Elizabeth said. She chose a tea bag from the wooden box he'd also set on the table. “So is this something that happens by mistake? Surely you can't control such a thing.”

“You absolutely can control it.” He poured near-boiling water into each cup, drowning their three different tea bags. “Like I said the last time you were here, bees pollinate in a three mile radius. That's the maximum. Many times it's much less.”

“Like your own backyard?”

“Exactly. Many amateur beekeepers have elaborate gardens for the express use of their bees. So, if you were so inclined, you could plant one full of rhododendrons.”

Elizabeth used a spoon to press down on her tea bag, watching the water become darker. “Okay, but what about stupidity? Do you think someone intended to make this honey poisonous? Maybe someone has a garden full of rhododendrons and doesn't know they are dangerous.”

"I suppose it's possible that a novice beekeeper could

make that mistake, but there are references to this in every guide you can buy on the market. It's not a secret. Any half-serious beekeeper would be aware of this." He drank his tea without removing the bag. "We're talking about a murderer though. That's evidence right there that it was intentional."

"That's true," she said, wrapping the tea bag around her spoon to squeeze out every last bit, then placing it on a napkin beside the mug. She added milk and sugar, pretending the honey wasn't there.

Mulrohney absentmindedly wiped the table in front of him with a napkin, even though it was still clean. "This isn't something new. There have been stories of 'mad honey' all throughout history. Around the time of Caesar, one of Rome's biggest enemies, King Mithridates used it to his advantage. He fed it to Pompey's invading army, and, once they were in a drugged stupor, Mithridates picked them off like flies."

"So it's not necessarily fatal?" she asked.

"No. In Turkey, it's often consumed as a drug." He tipped his cup to his mouth, draining the contents in one gulp. "Among other things, it causes a slow, irregular heartbeat. The biggest danger comes from either consuming too much or giving it to someone with a pre-existing heart condition."

James finally took out his tin, having barely touched his tea. "Do you mind, Mulrohney?"

He waved his hand encouragingly. "Please, make yourself at home."

The tin popped open and James pinched a small amount. "So tell me the really good news. Are rhododendrons easier to track than most stuff?"

"They are, considering they aren't native to Florida.

And I can do you one better. The honey also contains *Melaleuca*."

"What is that?"

"It's a tree that was introduced to the Everglades that has since become an aggressive and invasive weed. The University of Florida's Institute of Food and Agricultural Sciences keeps very careful track of the spread of *Melaleuca*, with very detailed maps of where it's been found."

"So all I have to do is consult them—"

"I already did it," Mulrohney said proudly. "I couldn't help myself. I had a fun day playing detective. First I called IFAS, and then I spoke to someone from the Florida Exotic Pest Plant Council. And in the end, I got you two good options."

"May I see?"

He hopped up and retrieved a map from a nook next to the kitchen. He removed their mugs and the condiments, then laid it out on the table. "Based on all of my research, the honey probably came from one of these two areas. One is more of a neighborhood, and the other is more rural. So if you have any idea which is more likely, you could save yourself some time."

"Thank you, Mulrohney," James said. "You really went above and beyond. Although I think the two of you may be getting ahead of yourselves. So let's say we do find out where the honey came from—how is that going to help us?"

Elizabeth frowned. "What if the place he gets the honey from is *his* apiary? It could even be located at his home. He would never think we'd be able to trace it back to him."

Mulrohney nodded. "Honey isn't the kind of thing that's easy to steal from someone else's turf. Beekeeping takes a lot of equipment and time. If the sample had been dirty, shown a lot of honeycomb pieces and bits of propolis, then I might be able to believe he did a 'smash and grab,' so to speak. This stuff is clean, the product of an experienced beekeeper."

James nodded. "Okay, I think we need to talk to Nick about this before we proceed any further. No need to go on a wild good chase."

"I thought you were interested in this line of investigation."

"I just don't want to be sidetracked from more traditional footwork. We need to do more interviews with the victims' families."

"All right," Elizabeth said with a sigh, standing up in the warm kitchen, but reluctant to leave its peace. "We'll talk to Nick."

"I REALLY DON'T WANT to talk about work right now." Nick had gotten to the vacant neighbor's house before she had, and he had made himself comfortable in the front bedroom. He'd picked up his laptop at some point during the day and had it in front of him, propped up on a TV tray table. "I have a movie on that we can watch, and some soda and chips in the kitchen."

"There are more important things than movies right now," she said, kicking off her shoes. "I wanted to talk to you about a few things."

"You need to have a balance," he said, not looking at her. "If you don't, you'll never survive in this job. Trust me."

"You're older and wiser?"

"Well, I'm wiser."

"Ha ha." She sat on the carpet next to him. "The arrogant Nick returns. I missed him."

Pressing a few buttons on the computer, he brought up the movie. "So do you want me to get the snacks now?"

She tucked her toes under the sleeping bag. "Is finding out where the honey came from a waste of time?"

"Let's talk about that tomorrow."

"What's the big deal if we talk about it now?" she pressed, trying to keep the whine out of her voice.

"Because it isn't necessary. I want us to have two work-free hours."

She didn't want to reward him by spending the night with him after he was so bossy, but she didn't have any other place to go. And if she were being honest, there probably wasn't a better way to relieve her stress.

THE THIRD BODY was found in a vacant apartment in a building near seventy-first and Biscayne. It was called in anonymously from a nearby payphone—probably by some dealer who figured that leaving the body where it was would be bad for business.

To Elizabeth, it almost felt as though Nick had known this would happen. Instead of getting a chance to discuss the case and what steps she might take next, she was at another crime scene. At that moment, the honey didn't seem very important to her, either. Another woman was dead because they had failed to solve the case.

James parked on the street. Elizabeth had two

thoughts simultaneously: first, that she was glad to have a partner, and second, that they'd be lucky if their unmarked vehicle was still there when they got back. She didn't need to look around the neighborhood much; it was the same area she drove through every night on her way home. It was the kind of place you could buy a car battery on the street corner and where most intersections had an amputee in a wheelchair holding up a grammatically incorrect plea for money written on the side of an old cardboard box. Where most people pressed the auto-lock button in their car twice just in case.

Before she became a cop, she hadn't even realized how much low-income housing was tucked behind Maybel's Discount Thrift. The rundown apartment buildings stretched out on either side of Biscayne Boulevard and all along the bay. Like most parts of Miami, someone was probably trying to buy all of it so they could tear it down and build high-rise condos that no one could afford.

James walked close to her side. "The apartment was vacant?"

"Technically." A teenager shot past on a child's bike and Elizabeth jumped back a step into the street. She'd been so intent on her task that she hadn't even heard him coming. "The place is vacant, but the landlord said that he's never been able to keep people out. Who knows who's been camping out there?"

"So much for preserving evidence."

The ground was unpaved and marked with puddles. Storms had raged all night, letting up politely before the business day started. The sky above was still swollen with dark clouds, but it was hanging back, waiting for the right moment to let go. Elizabeth let

James walk ahead of her, entering the dark interior of the building, while she swiveled one hundred and eighty degrees, trying to be aware of everything and everyone around her.

James didn't yell out any warnings or fall in a hail of gunfire, so Elizabeth entered the building behind him. The lobby was poorly lit, with only two overhead fixtures casting light down toward the peeling linoleum floor. Someone had left their garbage in the corner, flies hovering above the pile of Save-A-Lot grocery bags. There was an elevator with even dimmer lighting and a broken floor indicator overhead. Elizabeth saw a door propped open to the left. "Stairs?"

With a disparaging look at the elevator, he said, "I think that would be wise."

They entered the stairwell and were immediately assaulted by the strong smell of urine.

"Nice," James said, shoving his mouth full of chew in retaliation.

Elizabeth nodded, careful not to touch the railing. She climbed the stairs behind him. On the second landing, they had to climb over an unconscious half-naked man clutching a bottle of St. Ides. Elizabeth was grateful for that bottle of liquor. It meant they didn't have to check for a pulse or poke him with a stick. She practically jumped the stairs next to him, worried that he would suddenly grab her ankle and pull her down like a monster in a campy Halloween movie. She patted her gun and took a deep breath. Just making sure it was still there.

The unit they were looking for was on the third floor. The entire door to the landing was missing. They stepped through the splintered frame and onto what might have once been a rough industrial carpet. Now it was practically gone, worn down to the concrete and even burned away in some spots. Elizabeth grimaced and led the way to Apartment Thirty-Three. Somewhere down the hall a baby was wailing, and her pulse ratcheted up a few notches.

They were greeted by one of the uniformed officers who'd responded first and had secured the scene. He was on guard in the hall, his arms crossed. Behind him, the number thirty-three was drawn on the door in Sharpie marker. "Fiorello's already inside."

The door didn't latch properly, and it swung loosely in the frame. She and James went inside.

It smelled awful. James made a face worthy of a caricature. Elizabeth got about half a whiff of it: more urine, the smell of rotten food, and a slight undertone of human remains. Then she quickly snapped on a cheap surgeon's mask and started breathing through her mouth. It muffled her voice as she said, "At least the body hasn't been here that long."

"He's not wasting any time in building up his body count, is he?"

The victim was lying in the corner of the room. Once again, there was no blood or any sign of obvious blunt trauma. Just a bruised neck and frightening, bulging eyes. She had dark hair—almost black—just like Karina and Alice. And she was young, with a slender body. Elizabeth stepped closer, wondering if she was truly seeing what she thought she saw.

The honey was spilling out of the girl's mouth, running down her cheeks and pooling on the floor behind her head. There was much more of it—though Elizabeth couldn't imagine why—and, in consequence, the insect activity was worse. Aside from the ever-present ants, the apartment had cockroaches and flies.

A large brown roach scurried toward her, and Elizabeth changed direction. Nick came out of one of the bedrooms.

"Here's what we know," Nick said immediately. "This apartment is supposed to be vacant. No matter how big the lock is that the landlord puts on the door, it gets broken, and sooner or later, crack heads and vagrants are making this their home away from home."

"This girl's definitely no crack head."

"Doesn't look like one to me. Upon initial observation, she doesn't have track marks or any other indicators of drug use. She could be a bored college student experimenting with the dark side. A lot of drugs get sold in this apartment building, and if she was away from her regular dealer and really craving a hit..."

"Except that we have the honey in the mouth, just like Karina and Alice, and their deaths had nothing to do with drugs."

"That we know of," James said.

“Anything interesting in the other rooms?”

“Just a bunch of syringes, empty bottles, and fast food wrappers,” Nick said.

“Sounds like James's car.”

James shook his head. “*Our* car.”

Elizabeth walked the apartment, taking it all in. The floor was wood, comprised of an old collection of mismatched boards. The kind rich suburbanites put in their kitchens and called "rustic." Around the victim, the wood glistened with honey, and countless insects were entombed in the goop. Elsewhere the wood was rough and dull. If you walked across it barefoot, you'd probably get a splinter.

There was no furniture, but there were a few crates and boxes that might have substituted for tables and chairs for the squatters. One of the floorboards near the makeshift furniture seemed to stand out. Elizabeth crouched to take a closer look. "Hey, guys, look at this."

James came closer, while Nick handled something with the uniformed cops outside.

"Doesn't this look like an 'X'?" she asked.

"Like 'X marks the spot?'" He squinted. "Maybe. The grooves look pretty deep."

"Let me borrow your knife." After he passed it over, she inserted the tip of the knife into one of the lines forming the X. "It's deep. This looks intentional to me, not the kind of scratches you get from moving furniture."

"Here's another one. This is an arrow." He traced a sharp V with his finger. "It's right next to the X—"

"As if they're both pointing to the same place. Do you think…?" Elizabeth jammed the knife into the edge of the floorboard and, with a squeaky back and forth motion, tried to pry it up.

"Here, let me. It doesn't look like it's nailed down. It's just stiff." He took over and worked the knife all around the board until he'd weakened it. Finally, it was loose, and they pulled it up.

Her eyes immediately fell on a small box tucked between the studs. "Jackpot."

James leaned close. She could feel his breath on her shoulder and the moist smell of tobacco.

Elizabeth carefully lifted the lid of the box and then frowned when she saw what all of their hard work had produced. "It's a toy car."

James took the box and, without touching the toy, took a closer look. "One of those little Matchbox cars. I used to have dozens of these."

It was a red sports car, surprisingly shiny after being

in the floor, and it looked vintage. "Well, that was a waste."

"You never know," James said. "Our killer could be a collector. Maybe he hides one at each scene. We should get the whole thing fingerprinted."

"He already leaves the honey as his signature, but we'd better put it through the usual tests." Elizabeth stood up, her thighs aching.

She looked over to the victim, staring down at her gruesome remains. The honey was important. She was sure of it.

It was *all* about the honey.

GETTING information on the third victim was quick, as her fingerprints were in the system. An hour after they left the slum, they had her name. A few hours after that, they had her life story according to her adoptive mother.

Rachel Gomez had been a communications major at the University of Miami. According to her closest friends, she had liked to party. She had black hair streaked with deep scarlet, and more than the average amount of distinguishing marks. She had a rainbow tattoo on her lower back, and a dolphin curling around her pierced navel. She had a good body and liked to show it off. Her parents revealed that Rachel's enviable figure was a recent acquirement.

Rachel had only gone missing two nights ago. There was only a week to go before the fall semester began, and she'd wanted to make the most of it. A different club every night, according her friends. Two days ago, her partners in crime had had enough of the alcohol and ecstasy. A weeklong hangover couldn't be very enjoyable. Rachel still wanted to have fun, and she went out by herself.

Elizabeth and James did everything they could to figure out where she had been last, but Rachel hadn't used any of her credit cards and she hadn't gone to any of her usual haunts. The only thing they could surmise was that the killer had picked her up at a random bar, just like Karina.

As they were heading back to the station, a call came in from the crime scene unit.

"I got a match on one of the blood samples from the Roosevelt," Michael said. She could hear his enthusiasm through the phone.

"Which sample?" Elizabeth fumbled with her phone and nearly dropped it onto the floor of the car, unable to believe they actually had a lead on anything.

"From the glass picture frames."

"And? Whose blood is it?" Elizabeth asked.

"Dave Jackson."

Shaking her head, she finished up the call.

"So?" James asked. "What is it?"

"You're not going to believe this..."

CHAPTER 11

When they picked up Dave, he did a great job of acting like an unfairly persecuted victim. He didn't go so far as to resist coming with them, but he sure kept up a constant whine from the backseat during the drive to the station.

They got him comfortable in the interrogation room, as per the captain's instructions, and sat across from him in two chairs that were far more comfortable than the rickety metal one he was sitting on. All three chairs were bolted to the ground.

Elizabeth got things started. "We found your blood at a crime scene."

"The one at the house?" he asked, eyes wide. "That can't be."

"No, it was actually at another crime scene that was linked to the one you were found at. We have reason to believe that whomever is guilty of that crime is guilty of the other. Your presence at the house didn't exactly thrill us, and now we have biological evidence that you were at the location where another young woman was killed."

"This is crazy. You know why I was hiding in that closet: I didn't want you to see the pictures I took. I'm no more guilty than any of those guys." He flattened his palms on the table. "And I have no idea what you're talking about! My blood isn't anywhere except in my body. Where did I supposedly kill someone now?"

"Have you ever been to the Roosevelt Hotel?" James asked him.

"Is that where you're saying I killed someone?"

Elizabeth nodded. "A young woman was killed and, as I said, your blood was discovered in the vicinity."

He gnawed on the back of his knuckles, his eye sockets appearing shadowed and sunken with the way the recessed light in the ceiling shone slightly behind him.

"There's an abandoned level there. They stopped renovating it years ago, and left it that way."

"Fine," Dave said. "I've been there. I definitely didn't kill anyone though."

"This doesn't look good, Dave."

"It's on the list," he said with a nonchalant shrug. "So where did you find my…"

She watched him mull something over, thinking so intently that his forehead was wrinkled like a ruched gown. So she waited.

Finally, he said, "I know exactly what happened. I cut myself on some glass in one of the old hotel rooms. There's this stash of old pictures. I mean, I can't believe the hotel hasn't taken them and preserved them, but they haven't. They're just lying there collecting dust. It's a travesty, but you know…*take nothing but pictures.*"

"And?"

"One of the frames gave me a nasty cut." He reached across the table and showed her a scar on his hand. "See?"

James shook his head. "So you say, but—"

"When do you think I killed this woman?"

Elizabeth gave him the date.

Dave pulled out an iPhone, placed it flat on the table, and started up a calendar application. He scrolled back to the date in question and slid the phone over to her with a triumphant grin on his face. "Look: I was in jail that night. Ha!"

James frowned. "That didn't come up in our search."

"Did you check other states? I was in Detroit. A stupid security guard called the police on me and—well, you know. They threw me in with the drunks and prostitutes. I got out the next day. So there you go. I have an alibi."

"Doesn't everyone." Elizabeth rolled her eyes. "So when was the last time you were at the hotel?"

"Definitely not since then. Actually, I heard there was a bee infestation on that entire floor. From what I understand, no one is going to that site anymore. I might have ignored the warning. I mean, what are a few bees? Since I'd been there a couple times already, I put it on my do-not-go list."

"'A few bees?' Try thousands."

"Guess I made the right decision."

She pushed away from the table. "You're going to have to wait here until we confirm your alibi with the Detroit PD."

As soon as she walked out of the interrogation room and saw Nick, she knew he was ready to blow up. She steered Nick and James into an empty break room before Nick could get started on his rant.

"We've had a lot of bad luck, Nick," James said. "It's been a roller coaster."

The break room they used was the older, less popular one in the station. It was small and cramped, but at that moment it was perfect. Elizabeth shut the door behind the three of them and every sound from outside was muffled into a calming white noise.

"I just can't believe this keeps happening," James said. "We get leads, but they don't go anywhere."

"And each of these victims has been hard enough to track as it is," she added. "Clearly, he chooses party girls. Probably intentionally. The kind of women whose disappearance might go unnoticed."

"Exactly. So how would he know that?"

It was really coming down outside, and a leak in the corner of the ceiling was dripping water into a rusty bucket. The metallic strike of each drip echoed the beating of Elizabeth's heart. "Maybe the killer knows these women. It doesn't have to be random."

"We have to go back and speak to everyone," Nick said. "Friends and family. Maybe these women knew each other."

James's chair creaked loudly as he turned in it. "Right. At the same time, even if the killer knew all of them, they might not have known each other."

"Who would be in that position? A bartender, a DJ, a bouncer?" Nick asked.

"Karina was definitely taken from the Roosevelt Hotel bar, and the others..."

"We don't know where they were taken from. It's possible they were at the Roosevelt, as well."

Nick tugged on his tie, making it shift to the left.

"Take pictures of the victims to the bartender. And get security footage for the entire time period around when Alice and Rachel went missing."

"Okay," James said, making a note of it on his phone.

"Let's not get our hopes up, though," Nick said. "He would have had to travel with two of the women at the same time for this scenario to work out. Even if he's a charming guy that they would go with willingly, the route from the Roosevelt to Seventy-FirstStreet is a half-hour drive. Why would they ever agree to that?"

The tin of chewing tobacco came out, as expected. James hadn't even tried to resist this time. "It could be as simple as him claiming they were going to his house. He could say he lived anywhere."

Elizabeth shook her head. "I can't imagine any woman being okay with walking into that slum Rachel was killed in."

"He could have kept up the game until the very minute he parked," James said. "Who would have paid any attention to a woman screaming in that neighborhood?"

"All right. Look into it." Nick frowned. "It's not like we have any better ideas."

"Don't be so pessimistic," Elizabeth told him.

"CSU has a whole new crime scene to lift evidence from," James said. "Maybe that will result in something."

"The evidence is useless without a suspect," Nick pointed out.

Elizabeth grabbed an empty styrofoam cup from the stack, squeezing it until a little tear appeared at the rim. "I also have the honey thing."

"That's a long shot."

She tried not to get angry. "I don't know about that. At two of the three scenes, it wasn't just the honey.

There were bees present, as well. That would suggest some kind of connection to beekeeping. The honey isn't something that stands alone."

"Fine. *Maybe*," Nick admitted grudgingly.

"He's comfortable around bees," she continued. "We aren't so sure about the hive at the hotel, but he absolutely had to work around them when he lifted Alice onto the apiary."

"I just don't want you wasting too much time on it."

James nodded.

Nick was looking at the water bucket. "And did you see the news? Another goddamn hurricane is coming. We just got over the last one."

"I know," Elizabeth said. "It just doesn't feel like we have enough time."

"All right, I think for the rest of today, we split up. James goes to the Roosevelt, I go on a tour of the victims' homes to see if I can learn anything new, and Elizabeth goes honey-dipping."

James hitched up his suit pants and buttoned his jacket, looking anxious and distracted. "Let's hope at least one of us comes up with something."

And so Elizabeth left the station in her own car, with the two maps Patrick had prepared for her on the passenger seat. At least she could stop for coffee for the second time that day without James rolling his eyes at her.

ELIZABETH CHOSE the residential neighborhood on a hunch. Nick probably would have made her write a report on how and why she chose one location over the other. Fortunately, she was flying solo.

Since Patrick had circled a general area, she parked near the outskirts and toured the area on foot. It was a good time for it, too. The sidewalks were damp and there were puddles in the street, but the rain had let up, leaving behind a comfortable, albeit humid, temperature. The sky was cloudy and the sun was steadily dropping. She planned to make good use of the last couple hours of daylight.

The homes had large lots, far larger than she was used to seeing in Miami. On every street, there were signs of new wealth creeping in, a sharp contrast to the homeowners who'd been living there for decades. You could see it in the extensive renovations and brand new homes that had been built on the foundations of simple ranchers, often right next door to much older homes that still had shingled roofs and iron scrollwork over the windows.

It was a lot quieter than she'd expected, and her hopes of finding someone to casually speak to quickly evaporated. When she'd gotten almost to the end of one particular block, she heard a door slam behind her, from the direction she had come from. Elizabeth turned around to see whom it was, not wanting to resort to knocking on doors.

A woman was walking down the path in front of a house. She stepped carefully, wearing a voluminous housedress. She stopped a few yards from the sidewalk where Elizabeth stood. "This is the second time you've walked by here. Can I help you with something?"

"Actually, yes." To save time with the inevitable questions that would come next, Elizabeth pulled out her identification. In her line of work, nosy neighbors had always been both a blessing and a curse. "I'm looking for someone in this neighborhood who has an apiary in their backyard. You wouldn't happen to know anyone like that, would you?"

"I've lived here longer than you've been alive. If anyone knows anything about this neighborhood, it's me," she said, pursing her lips and shoving her hands into the pockets of her dress.

"Okay, great," Elizabeth said. "So who keeps bees?"

"No one does right now, thank goodness," she said. "They look for places to drink, you know. That's what used to happen with my pond. All the bees would descend upon it like they were dying of thirst. That wouldn't have happened if the person with the bees had offered them a proper water source. Amateurs."

Elizabeth nodded. "So someone *used to* keep bees. How long ago?"

"The last time I heard anything like that must have been...oh, I don't know, twelve years ago?"

It fit with the age of the bottle they'd pieced together in the lab. Of course, they couldn't prove which apiary the honey had come from if it had long since been destroyed. "Do you know whose it was?"

"Gillian, at the end of the block. Been living there going on twenty years. It's the old house on the corner, next to the one with the shell lawn."

"Shell lawn?"

"You know, when instead of grass they've just landscaped the entire yard with crushed seashells? It's disgraceful," she said, shaking her head.

"Oh, right. Well thank you very much for the information!"

The woman nodded carefully, as though she was still suspicious, watching Elizabeth as she walked away.

~

THERE WAS no car in the driveway, but there was a garage with a severely rusted door. Elizabeth walked up the path to the front door. As she knocked on the door, she absorbed the surroundings and made notes of everything. The lawn was mowed with the edges neatly trimmed, but it was lacking the freshness that characterized the neighbors' yards. Even the so-called "shell yard" seemed more carefully maintained. The grass had too many patches of dirt, and the whole thing was crisp, dry, and sparse. She couldn't say that the property had been let go, but it clearly wasn't lovingly maintained.

There were two lovely stone urns on the porch where she stood, but the plants that had once bloomed inside them were crumbling over the sides onto the concrete. The windows flanking the door were old jalousies, and traces of dried-out masking tape were yellowing on the glass in a tribute to past hurricane seasons. Elizabeth tried to peer inside as she knocked, but the window was cloudy with caked-on grime. There were no sounds coming from inside.

She left the porch, a gust of wind blowing a smattering of sharp raindrops into her face. Though the clouds above were full and black, it still hadn't resumed raining, and she walked into the backyard.

A man was crouching near the weathered fence, partially concealed by a pine tree. He was yanking weeds with angry precision and depositing them into a black garbage bag at his feet.

She cleared her throat. "Excuse me? Do you live here?"

He looked up from his work, but before he could answer, he saw her and the words seemed to get stuck in his throat. It was George Hamish.

Elizabeth was speechless, herself. *What the hell?*

Finally, she said, "I'm here to see Gillian." No way was George Hamish's popping back into the investigation a coincidence. But no way was she going to let on that he had just become suspect *numero uno*...again.

"Very funny," he said, and bent to twist the garbage bag closed. He let out a weary groan as he rose to his feet, gingerly touching his hamstring.

"Funny? How is that funny?"

"*I'm* Gillian. I know it has pretty much become a feminine name, but it used to be quite masculine. Unfortunately you can't argue with the majority, so now everyone knows me as George."

She stood there dumbly for a moment, not wanting to give herself away. She had no idea a man could be called Gillian. She wasn't sure what was worse: looking stupid or looking like she had been trying to insult him. What the hell, she'd go with the insult. "Well, perhaps it's time you applied for the change. Otherwise, you'll be hearing it all your life."

"So what brings you by?"

"I'd like to ask you some more questions." She wanted to ask him if what was in the bag could possibly be a purple, bell-shaped flower, but thought better of it.

"Fine, go ahead." He looked up at the sky as though there wasn't much time to chat. "I'm no longer a suspect, right?"

"Of course not."

He nodded. "So what did you want to know?"

"I've been told that you used to have an apiary." She looked around the yard to see if there was any sign of it, but twelve years was a long time.

"What does that have to do with anything?"

She shook her head slowly. "Could you just answer the question?"

"Yes, I had one. It was a long, long time ago."

"How long ago?"

"I don't know. Ten years?"

She leaned closer to him. "What made you get rid of it?"

He shrugged, then tied the drawstrings on the garbage bag and walked to the front of the house. "I just got tired of the extra work."

She followed him, watching him toss the bag on top of a heap at the side of the road. His garbage was now abandoned property. She could have grabbed it right then and there, but she preferred not to tip him off.

He looked at her, waiting, then said, "I really need to go. Have to get ready for work."

"Oh, that's right. The night shift. Please, go ahead."

George walked straight into his house without looking back, and Elizabeth took one last longing glance at the garbage bag. But no, she'd have to come back. It was better that way, and would save a lot of embarrassment if she were wrong about what he'd been tearing out of his yard. But really, even without rhododendrons, he'd had an apiary. And what were the chances that the man who'd tried to pick up Victim One at the Roosevelt bar on the night that she had been murdered just happened to have once kept bees…and in one of the two areas Patrick Mulrohney claimed the honey had come from?

Elizabeth didn't believe in coincidences.

THERE WERE MORE people at the urgent care center at that hour, and Sandra was speaking to one of them when Elizabeth walked in. She'd sped the entire way to

Aventura, even though she didn't expect George to leave his house for at least another half-hour.

She waited a moment until the patient walked away, and then approached the window before Sandra could slide it closed. "Can I speak to you for a minute? I'll come around."

Sandra nodded.

Elizabeth moved past the door that closed off the waiting area, turned, and then went through another door that led into the room where they did billing and scheduling. Another woman was working on a computer nearby. Elizabeth whipped out her badge and asked her to give her a moment alone with Sandra.

Sandra didn't move from her seat behind the reception window. "How can I help you today?"

After pressing the button on a handheld digital recorder, Elizabeth said, "I'll be recording this conversation. Is that all right with you?"

"Sure."

"Okay. I want to talk to you about George and the night you said he was here."

"What about it?"

Sitting in a rolling chair, Elizabeth scooted closer to Sandra and looked her in the eye. "He wasn't really here, was he?"

"He was here," she said, blinking rapidly. "Didn't his timecard prove it?"

"That's easy enough to fake. He called you and asked you to scan it for him."

"No."

"Is he really worth going to jail for?" Elizabeth leaned forward, elbows on her knees. "You know, I don't mean to threaten you. Maybe I just need to explain the whole situation so you can make the right decision."

Sandra swallowed, her lips pressed together tightly.

"George is a suspect in the murder of three women. He was seen—by witnesses and on tape—with one victim on the night she was killed. He violently raped this young woman, then strangled her until her eyes practically popped out of her head."

Sandra took her glasses off and cleaned them on her shirt. "He could never do something like that."

"How do you know? Do you think people ever suspect that someone they know might be a brutal killer? Of course not. Yet it happens *all the time.*"

"He's a quiet man—"

"Sandra, even if you don't believe him to be a murderer, one thing that is an undeniable fact is that George isn't such a shy guy. He himself admits that he picked up a woman in a bar and tried to have sex with her in a dirty stairwell." She glanced at the clock on the wall. "And, by the way, we looked at his phone records. He called you that night after the murder had been committed. I would strongly advise against risking your life to protect him."

"Look, he did come in to work. He really did," she said, but her hand was shaking as she put her glasses back on, and she wasn't making eye contact.

"He might have come in, but not when the timecard said he did."

Sandra nodded, frowning in a way that made her entire face wrinkle. "He got here maybe an hour after he'd called me to ask me to scan it. He told me he hadn't done anything wrong and that it was unlikely that anyone would even ask me about it. If they ever did, however, I would have to lie."

"Why would you do that for him?"

Sandra lowered her voice to a whisper. "I slept with him a few months ago."

"And he was that good?"

"No," she said, scornfully, then held up her left hand. "He said he would tell my husband if I didn't do this for him. I love my husband more than anything. He can't ever know about what happened. George was just a stupid mistake."

Elizabeth turned off the recorder and stood up. "If George finds out about this conversation and does a runner, I will personally arrest you for obstruction."

"I'm not going to tell him anything. I swear."

Elizabeth hurried out. She had one last thing she needed to do.

CHAPTER 12

She didn't go so far as to put on a black turtleneck and leather pants, but she did park a block away from George's house. She walked the distance quickly, the thrill of closing in on the end lightening her step. If there were rhododendrons in that bag, she would dance in the street.

Her gaze fell on the trash bags the moment they were within view. They were nicely placed on the street, legally public property. The large black bag was on top, only partially filled. She approached the house, looking for any lights and listening to every sound. Anything that would indicate George had unexpectedly decided to stay home. There was nothing, and she exhaled into the wind.

She walked casually and gently lifted the top bag. With the bag in hand, she walked slowly back to her car. Even before she got there, she was untying the bag with shaking hands. Then, using the light of a street lamp, she peered inside and pulled out a good handful of the weeds.

She spent a moment holding them in front of her, turning them this way and that, purple petals falling onto the wet asphalt. There was no doubt. They were rhododendrons.

Dropping them back into the bag, she realized she'd stopped walking, her shadow being cast onto the street. Then another shadow appeared beside her.

She dropped the bag and reached for her gun. She whirled in the direction of the shadow, her gun completely out of its holster before she saw who was addressing her. It was her old friend in the floral house-dress. Elizabeth quickly holstered her gun.

The woman picked up the garbage bag, completely unconcerned that she'd just had a deadly weapon pointed at her. "Going through the trash?"

"You shouldn't sneak up on people," Elizabeth replied and tried to retrieve the bag.

The lady yanked it close to her body and glared at its contents. "Yard waste," she said with disgust. "What do you want with this?"

"It's really none of your concern." She held out her hand.

The old lady handed it back with a shrug. "I called your department the last time you came around here. They weren't aware of any detectives investigating our neighborhood."

"And?"

This seemed to take her aback. "Well, what are you up to? I don't think Gillian Hamish would appreciate you stealing his garbage, garbage though it is."

"Why do you call him Gillian?"

"That's his name! It's on his tax records and I'm sure his birth certificate. You don't get to change your name just because you don't like it."

Actually, many people did, but the woman probably meant it from some kind of respect-of-ones-family standpoint. "How do you even know this is George's trash?" Elizabeth asked.

"The rhododendrons, of course," she said haughtily. "He's been fighting a losing battle with them for years."

Elizabeth looked the old lady over from the curlers in her salt-and-pepper hair to the Isotoners on her feet. "And why do you think he hates them so much?"

"Probably because his wife loved him them. Only a couple of weeks after her heart gave out, he was out there ripping them to shreds. Susan loved rhododendrons, had them planted all over the yard. She was from some place up north where they're more common."

"Was she young?"

"Yes, it was a real shame. Nice woman, from what I recall."

"How soon after that was the apiary gone?"

"I don't quite know, since I don't associate with Gillian and we don't share news of that sort, but it was definitely that same year."

"Thank you. You've been very helpful."

"Come by anytime if you want to know what's what. We'll have a cuppa." She started to turn away. "Wait a second. You never told me what you're up to."

"No, I didn't, but by tomorrow, I think the whole neighborhood will know."

Elizabeth told Nick everything the minute she walked through the door. He was thrilled. He showed her exactly how happy he was in the bedroom, the kitchen, and even the shower.

"How long until we can get the warrant and a suitable team in place?" she asked after collapsing breathlessly onto a flannel blanket.

"Early afternoon at the latest," he said, taking a long swig from a bottle of water and then passing it to her.

She drank, stretched languorously, and closed her eyes. "So by this time tomorrow, it will all be over."

NICK BANGED ON THE DOOR. "POLICE!"

Elizabeth flinched, thinking she'd heard a sound from inside, but it was so hard to tell. The storm in the Atlantic was quickly approaching, blanketing South Florida with a continuous downpour. It was only two o'clock in the afternoon, but it was as dark as a summer evening. She backed up and tried to get a look through the windows. Between the built-up dirt and the old window screens, it was impossible to even see shadows. Then she looked at the rest of the team, in place around the entire property. There was no escape. Worst-case scenario was that he wasn't home.

It seemed Nick might have heard a sound, too. "George Hamish? This is the police. Open the door slowly with both hands in front of your body. We want this to go smoothly. It's in your best interest."

Again, they waited. Elizabeth's heart upped its tempo. She took a labored breath. The silence was suffocating her.

Nick signaled to the guys with the compact battering ram. "Okay, George. We have a warrant to enter the premises. If you don't want to open the door, we're going to have to do it for you."

They got into position. With such an old door, all it

required was the right amount of force in the weak spots, and they were in. The frame of the door shattered, raining wood shards onto the porch. Nick led the way inside, gun held at the ready.

Elizabeth walked in behind him. Her gaze scanned the house. It showed the same lack of attention as the exterior of the property. The walls were covered in raffia wallpaper that was peeling at the edges. She'd bet that if one were to take down the paintings, there would be pale squares left on the walls. The house was cluttered with books, but it was too dark to make out any titles. There was a stone mantel with a few picture frames on display. In front of a photograph of a young, blonde woman was a jar of dark golden goo that shone in the dull light coming in through the broken door. Honey.

She looked at Nick and unspoken words flew between them. Where was George?

Three members of the team were about to fan out into the closed, shadowed areas of the home when a muffled footstep broke the silence. It came from out of the darkness at the end of the hall. She nodded to Nick, who nodded back with a grimace.

When she took a step forward, she felt his hand on her shoulder. Her entire body jerked, despite knowing it was him. She knew his heavy touch—would know it in pitch-blackness.

Nick shook his head and made a move in front of her. He was going to go in first.

Elizabeth turned to him and hoped he could read her fervent gaze as easily as she could his touch. She had to do this herself. She had to prove she could.

And maybe only because the decision had to be made quickly, Nick stepped aside.

With her heart beating in her throat, Elizabeth took careful steps down the hall. Her gaze darted into each shadow, stretching into the distance as much as humanly possible. It was as though all of her senses were tuned in to form a full picture of the room at the end of the hall, despite the harsh reality that she still could see nothing.

Unmoving, he was waiting for her in the darkness.

She heard the creak of a bedspring. She closed the distance rapidly, gun held at the ready.

The whites of his eyes glowed in the dark room for a split second before he turned to grab something on the bedside table. Something metal glinted in the ray of moonlight shining through a crack in the closed curtains. There was movement. He was coming for her.

Elizabeth shot off two rounds. They sparked in the near darkness. George fell backwards, hitting the corner of the bed frame and falling into a heap on the ground.

She gasped for air. Her reaction time was as quick as ever. Images of how Quinton Alvarez had fallen beat their way into her brain and she bit down on the inside of her cheek to keep her composure. It wasn't the same thing. It wasn't the same thing at all.

"Nick, the lights." Her voice came out hoarse.

As she stared at George's unmoving body, she heard Nick moving behind her. She heard the flick of a switch, but the room remained dark. Nick cursed bluntly and crossed the room. With his gun still trained on George, Elizabeth saw him fumble with the chain of a lamp on the bureau. Nick's body was reflected back at her in the dresser mirror. Then the room was bright.

Elizabeth blinked at the sudden light. As soon as the spots in front of her eyes began to recede, she focused on the man lying on the ground. Then she caught her breath and swallowed bile.

She'd hit him once in the chest and once in the neck. It wasn't a pretty sight. But it answered the question that was on everyone's mind. George was dead, and he wasn't coming back.

Nick nodded. "I saw that honey in the living room. This has been our guy all along. At least the victims' families won't have to suffer through a trial."

Elizabeth breathed deeply, trying to calm the rapid beating of her heart. It was done. Over. And they'd only gotten to this point thanks to her. She could go to sleep that night knowing that, at least when it came to George Hamish, no more young women would be killed. As she stared down at the body, it didn't feel the way it should have.

She felt defeated.

As Nick phoned the station to talk to the ME and the captain, Elizabeth stood frozen to the spot. Her two spent shells blinked up at her from the avocado shag carpeting. George looked accusingly at the ceiling.

He'd seemed lively enough when she'd spoken to him in life, but now he looked worn out. Wrinkled and supple, like an old leather handbag.

Elizabeth finally moved. She felt the fog descend around her. She crouched next to George's body and looked into his still-open eyes. A chill traversed up her spine.

This was her second time killing another human being, and she'd never even wanted the first.

~

"Come on now, Elizabeth. This isn't your first fatal shooting." Nick crouched next to her.

She felt his hand on the small of her back. "That's exactly my problem."

"He's a bastard and he deserved it. No one deserved it more than him."

Elizabeth took a deep breath. "How do we know it's him for sure? That he killed those women?"

He stood up and offered her his hand. "You saw the honey on the mantel. He used to have an apiary, in a location that fits perfectly. He was the last person seen with Karina Brookes. In a few days, we'll have this whole thing wrapped up."

She ignored his proffered hand. "I wish we could have just arrested him."

"It was a valid shooting. We all saw him pull that knife." He paused. "Wait a second…where is the weapon?"

His words jogged her memory, too, and she couldn't believe it had escaped her notice. Where was the item that she'd seen glinting ominously in the darkness?

George's arm was stretched above his body, partially concealed by a floral bed skirt. Elizabeth didn't want to get any closer to the body, no matter how obvious his lack-of-pulse was to all who were gathered, so she stood up and used her foot to push aside the fabric. It only took a little nudge, and his hand was visible. Lying against his palm, which was now flaccid in death, was a dull butter knife.

Nick squinted. "Is that blood?"

Elizabeth's gaze went to the bedside table, where there was a small plate. "Looks like jam. Probably strawberry."

He laughed.

Elizabeth turned and walked out of the room. This wasn't happening. Not again.

Nick was quick to follow her. "Don't be a girl, Stratton. Butter knife or machete, he was wielding it in a threatening manner. A butter knife in your eye, and you're dead. You did the right thing. If I had walked in ahead of you, I would have done the exact same thing."

She unzipped her vest. It had to be at least eighty-five degrees in there.

"James will talk some sense into you," Nick told her.

"I can't talk to him right now. I'm too embarrassed." The clutter of the house was oppressive. This man had led a sad life. If he wasn't the killer she sought, her actions had just added to the tragedy of his existence. Then again, maybe she'd done him a favor. "I need some air."

"Elizabeth?"

She wasn't sure where her partner had run off to, but she didn't much care. She paused on the threshold of the house. Police tape had already been stretched across the front of the porch, and the wind had blown it onto the wet concrete pathway. It waved at her with each gust, a bright flag in the looming darkness.

"Trust me on one thing, will you?" Nick said. "Once you get some rest, you'll realize that you're just in shock. You can't believe it's finally over, but it is."

She hoped to God he was right.

NICK STARTED to unknot his tie, working his fingers underneath the loop. "Feeling okay?"

"About?" Elizabeth pulled the fitted sheet over the

bottom end of the mattress, having to put her foot on the bed frame and yank to get enough leverage.

"Being back home. Sleeping in your bed again."

"George is dead and I don't believe in ghosts. When it comes down to it, it was just honey. I've put my foot in worse." It also helped that the moment they'd walked into the house, before Nick even had a chance to get out of his suit, they'd stripped the bed and flipped the mattress for good measure.

He dropped his tie on the plush chair in the corner of her bedroom, then proceeded to unbutton his shirt. His jacket had already been abandoned in the dining room. He looked so confident—arrogant, even—as he got undressed. He hadn't even asked her what she wanted. "I'm glad to hear that. I always knew you were tough."

"I was thinking about some stuff."

He was now wearing only his pants, loosely unbuttoned. "Like?"

She couldn't deny that he looked *very* good. So she looked away. "You've tried to get under my skin in the past, talking about Chris and what, apparently, *everyone* in the department knew."

"So you want to know what I know."

She nodded and turned away. She grabbed the folded flat sheet from the bureau and shook it open.

Nick grabbed the other end to help her, his muscles flexing attractively even with such a simple movement. "I knew you were banging him."

She felt like she'd been punched in the stomach. "You guessed?"

He gave an incredulous laugh. "No, he told me."

"Just out of morbid curiosity, is this something that Captain McQuinn is also aware of?"

"Absolutely. They're closer than anyone. Didn't you know that?"

"I had no idea."

"It's probably why McQuinn hates you. His friend had to go to a different department while you stayed here. I don't think he thinks it was very fair, and I don't think he likes having to deal with you."

That explained some things. She wasn't being paranoid if they really were out to get her. She plumped the pillows at the top of the bed, then gave up on the whole thing and sat down with a forlorn sigh. "What exactly did Chris tell you?"

"That he was banging you."

"Isn't there a better way of saying that?" She was facing the wall, while he was still on the other side of the bed. She didn't want to look at him.

Clearly, he hadn't gotten the memo. Nick walked around the bed and sat next to her. "I'm sorry. That's how your ex-partner always put it."

It was all running through her head, too quickly for her to catch each strand, but she thought she understood what he was saying. She swallowed, her mouth dry. "He shared intimate details, didn't he?"

"Yes."

"I knew he was an asshole, but I guess I didn't realize how much."

"If it makes you feel any better, it was all flattering."

"No, it doesn't make me feel better. Well, maybe a little." She laughed, a sad, pathetic little bark that was unsubstantial. Then she frowned again, realizing something else. "Does this big mouth of his extend to the night my life took a turn for the worse?"

"That the reason you didn't see Quinton Alvarez break into his ex-wife's house when you were supposed to be staked outside the entire night is because you were blowing Chris in the front seat of your car? Yeah, we all know." He touched her leg, high up on her thigh, and gently squeezed. "Honestly, I thought it sounded pretty hot."

She pushed his hand away, furious at Chris, furious at Nick, and furious at her body for betraying her. Because, despite their conversation and his wholly inappropriate comment, her entire body had tingled when Nick had touched her. "It's not hot that a woman is dead because of me."

"Hold on there just a second, Stratton." He scooted closer to her rather than farther away. "Let's get this straight. Mrs. Alvarez deserved our protection and it's terrible that she was killed. When you get involved with a man like Quinton Alvarez, you know there are going to be consequences. She liked the money and the glamor—regardless of how he was obtaining it—until he started preferring the company of his favorite girlfriend to her. So don't lose any sleep over it. You fixed the problem that same night."

"They say I shot too soon. Even you've said so—many times—that I'm trigger-happy. I think you're right."

"It's over. You need to move on. You've done a phenomenal job on this case. You're back in action and better than ever."

She shook her head. "No, that's not right. Look at how I shot George today. Again, finishing things prematurely. Unable to keep a level head under pressure."

"It's over," he repeated again and leaned over to kiss her on the neck. His lips moved slowly, gently over her skin.

A shiver went through her body, ending between her legs. "I was probably distracted by you."

"Did you think about it all day? What I was going to do to you tonight?"

Yes.

He continued to kiss her neck and put his hand on her thigh, slowly moving it higher as he kissed her.

Elizabeth tried to move away, but he held her tight. "I can't do this, Nick."

"You are *so* good at it though."

"I can't be with someone only for the sex, and I absolutely cannot be in a relationship with you. It would be the death of my reputation."

"How do you figure?"

"I was sleeping with Chris, and now I'm sleeping with you. Even if my relationship with Chris hadn't turned out as monumentally horrible as it did, it's still me being passed around from detective to detective in this department. How do you think that makes me look?"

He lowered her onto the bed, his heavy weight pushing her into the pillow top mattress. "Chris was an unfortunate mistake, but no one could blame you for being with me. I'm the alpha dog."

She turned her head away when he tried to kiss her. "Get over yourself."

"All I think about when I consider my colleague is whether or not they are good at their jobs." He reached down to adjust himself with a groan, his pants slipping down to his thighs. She saw him straining against his briefs, large and swollen.

Elizabeth gasped, feeling the warmth run through her body. She didn't have the willpower to kick him out that night. Maybe she *was* a slut. She wrapped her legs around his waist.

Nick looked down at her thoughtfully, finished with his arousing manipulations. "Do you want me to leave?"

"Yes," she said, tightening her legs around him.

"Elizabeth," he said, shaking his head. "What did your mother teach you about sending mixed messages?"

"Just finish what you were doing. Then we'll talk."

One thing she knew: being with Nick was nothing like being with Chris.

She was lying next to Nick and he was making her feel safe in a way that even closing the beekeeper case hadn't. Was there something about her that just needed to have a man at her side? Did it have more to do with Nick personally, or was he just a placeholder? No matter what, she was attracted to him like bees to honey.

CHAPTER 13

Elizabeth went back to George's house with James the next day. Even though their killer was now deceased, they needed a good case to support the events of yesterday. And the victims' families would want clear confirmation that they'd found the right guy. Everyone was working quickly, and there was a nervous energy in the air. The hurricane was predicted to hit that very night.

Nick was micromanaging a crime scene tech in the kitchen who looked like he was about to punch him in the face. "Make sure you test the grout. They always forget to scrub the hell out of the grout. See that right there?"

"Yes, I've got it!"

Elizabeth walked back into the living room and ran straight into Max. She immediately wiped the smile off of her face. "I'm really sorry for your loss."

He looked a bit stunned. "Was it you?"

"Was what me?"

He approached the mantel. The honey had already

been taken away, but the picture of the pretty blonde woman was still there. He touched the frame gently. "Are you the one who killed my father?"

"He had a weapon."

"So it *was* you." He didn't take his eyes off the silver framed photograph. "Don't lose any sleep over it. I won't."

"You mentioned that you and he weren't getting along. Why is that?"

"He killed my mother," he said, nodding at the picture, then exhaling loudly and turning away from the mantel.

"I was told she died of a heart problem."

"He told everyone that, but she only had a heart problem because of the honey he fed her every single day until she died. She got so sick and nobody could figure out why. She loved the fresh honey, and he'd bring her as much as she wanted."

Elizabeth followed him as he moved toward the bedroom. "Mad honey, right?"

"It was poisonous because of all the rhododendrons my father planted in the yard. Which was completely intentional. He wouldn't let me eat it, saying that my mother loved it so much that we needed to save every last bit for her."

"Why didn't you turn him in?"

"I'd never heard of mad honey back then. I finally put the pieces together after I read about it in a beekeepers' magazine. Even if I *had* known, I was thirteen years old. What would you have expected me to do?" He moved down the hall, clearly intending to enter his father's room.

"You shouldn't go in there," she said. "It might be upsetting."

“I just want to see for myself.”

James appeared beside Max. “Your father has already been transported to the morgue.”

“Oh. I hadn't realized.” He looked crestfallen as he walked back to the front of the house.

"Why did he want your mother dead?" Elizabeth asked.

"So he could run around with other women. I guess my mother was cramping his style. He sure made up for lost time after her death. He seemed to go after the ones who looked the least like my mother. Black hair, pale skin…"

"I guess he was a creature of habit,” she said. “So he got rid of the apiary after your mother died?”

"He *destroyed* it. In the most brutal way he could think of. Those bees had become my only friends." He shook his head and looked away. "I sound like an imbecile."

"No, go on."

"I just used to talk to them. There's this legend that says when someone in a household dies, you must inform the bees, or else. I stayed with my mother in the hospital until the very end, even after my father went home. When I finally got home, I went into the backyard to tell the bees what had happened, but the apiary had been torn apart. The bees were dead—many of them stomped on. It was awful."

James had been checking something on his phone, but looked up then, as though he'd realized something. “You said something about reading a beekeeper magazine. Do you keep bees, Max?”

"I had a small apiary until recently."

"What happened?" James asked.

"Colony collapse. It was just like when my father

killed them, but this time it was something else. Nobody knows what, exactly. Nature can be a bitch." He eyed the open door to the house. "Did you know that if all the bees in the world died, the human race might die out, as well?"

"I heard something like that."

"Something to think about when you're swatting them away."

Elizabeth pulled out her notebook and a pen. "Could you tell me where your apiary was?"

"It was in an orange grove," he said, then gave her the address. "It took me a long time to consider beekeeping after what my father did. I used to think that all those dead bees had cursed me."

Nick came out of the kitchen and looked at Max with raised eyebrows. "Hello," he said, holding out his hand.

Max backed away. "Listen, I need to get going. I have to figure out how I feel about all of this."

"So that's his son, huh?" Nick asked, the very moment after Max had exited onto the porch.

"Not exactly devastated over his father being dead," Elizabeth said.

"What a coincidence," Nick said, "Neither am I."

Elizabeth had had enough of the gloomy house. There was one thing she was certain of: she couldn't wait until all the evidence came back to conclusively prove that George had killed those three women.

THE CASE WOULDN'T BE complete until she checked out Max's apiary. It would be interesting to get a sample and compare it to the samples they already had.

There was also a part of her that wanted to make sure Max wasn't lying about anything. He had already lied to them once, after all.

She picked up Patrick on the way and he brought a large backpack with everything he might need to obtain the sample and take a good look at the apiary. If there had been full colony collapse, he told her, he might not need any special equipment.

Patrick led the way. "It will be near a source of water. Lots of sunlight would be best, so maybe something on a small hill?"

"You clearly haven't been in Florida long enough," she said. "No hills around here."

They walked around a large industrial building and came upon two men. They were both in full beekeeper garb—white from head to foot. They were speaking to each other in low tones and unloading some boxes from a trolley.

"Excuse me?"

One of the men turned to her. "Yes?"

"I'm Elizabeth Stratton." She flashed her badge. "I was wondering if I might ask you a few questions?"

"They always blame the bees," the second man said with obvious humor in his voice. "Poor, misunderstood bees."

"No, we're bee friends," Patrick said proudly.

The first man took off his hood and looked at Elizabeth. "Don't worry. It's safe. You can come closer."

"That's okay," she said, though she hadn't really meant to stay so far back. "I'm trying to locate an apiary. Its owner said that it's obsolete, but I wouldn't count on it. Have you seen anything? Especially anything that looks abandoned?"

The guy in the hood said, "No, nothing like that."

Then his friend said, "What about that apiary we found last month?"

"You mean that heap of driftwood?" He loaded the truck with clear plastic containers with chunks of honeycomb. "Ben's talking about something we saw when we were scouting locations. There was a ramshackle collection of frames—real amateur stuff. I assumed the landowner had tried to put it together himself as a weekend project."

"Were the bees still there? Was there any honey that you were aware of?"

"Only small amounts of both. It was a bad location to begin with, and quite a trek from the road. There were still some bees hanging around, but it was a disorganized hive. I'm sure there was some honey at the time, but I wasn't about to get involved, especially without speaking to the landowner."

"Did you ever ask him about it?"

"No."

"Could you find it again?"

He looked up at the dark clouds overhead. A gust of wind blew a damp leaf onto his white suit and it stuck. "I have a pretty good idea of where it was. I'd take you there now, but we have some more things we have to do before the hurricane hits. Maybe after the storm? I'll have to come back to check on things immediately anyway."

"Maybe you could give me an idea of where it might be and I could take a look today."

"So it's urgent, eh? I'll draw you a map."

THE WEATHER HAD WORSENED by the time Elizabeth and

Patrick got on their way. The orange blossoms on the trees were being ripped off by the wind. They rained down on her and littered the dark, foot-worn path that stretched between the trees. Something in the air sounded different, something she'd never been able to describe to her friends back home. When a storm was churning in the Atlantic, if you listened very carefully, you could hear it coming.

Referring to the crudely drawn map she carried, they took the path. Although there was a busy highway nearby, she felt that they were more alone the farther they walked through the trees. Soon, the road was far behind and they were surrounded on all sides by bright orange globes. Whoever had tended to this apiary in the past, would have had a long journey with their supplies.

She took a deep breath, savoring the freshness of the air. The windy weather seemed to whisk the smog of the city off of the ground, leaving behind only the scent of oranges and damp earth. After a lengthy walk during which she mentally laid out every piece of evidence she'd gathered so far, only to come up empty, she smelled something different.

Something was burning. She did a three-sixty, making two dusty circles in the dirt with the toes of her boots as she strained to see the sky above the trees. She would have heard about any large fires in the area, but the thought gave her little comfort.

"Smells like a serious smoker," Patrick said, breaking the silence. "Every beekeeper in South Florida is likely out today, doing the best they can to protect their hives."

After taking another quick look at the map, Elizabeth started to lead Patrick through the trees. The fumes were getting stronger by the minute, but never bad enough for her to want to turn around. As long as she could still see her hand in front of her face, she'd keep going.

She could taste burnt wood at the back of her throat as she and Patrick entered a clearing. Ahead of her was an area that sloped down towards another long row of orange trees. A hooded beekeeper was standing with his back to them. He was pumping smoke into the stacks of beehives. The smoky haze hovered between her and the man, and he didn't give any sign he was aware of her arrival.

"Is this the one?" Patrick asked softly. "He's really going overboard with the smoke."

The fumes seared the back of her throat and she couldn't prevent the automatic reflex. She coughed forcefully and the beekeeper turned his head sharply to one side.

Elizabeth stepped backward involuntarily and touched the handle of her gun. She stared at the man without saying anything, evaluating the situation. The sky had darkened considerably since she'd spoken to the other two men. They had seemed eager for the conversation. With this person, she almost felt like she should hang back, as though she'd be disturbing a private ritual.

"Aren't we going to speak to him?" Patrick pulled off his backpack. "Whew, I'm not used to walking so much."

"Sure, let's go." The smoke was only getting thicker in the air, the brisk wind doing little to disperse it. Her eyes burned and started to water, quickly obscuring her vision. She was forced to squeeze her eyes shut and she wiped them with the hand that wasn't on her gun. When she opened her eyes, the beekeeper was gone.

She took out her gun and pointed it toward the dilapidated apiary. Her arm twitched, her finger wobbling in front of the trigger. The trees had thick trunks that could easily hide a man. She looked all around the clearing, steadying her aim with both hands. *Steady, Elizabeth. Steady.*

"Stay right there, Patrick. This doesn't feel right." The closer she was to the center of the clearing, the better. Her phone was in her front pocket, its corner poking her beneath the curve of her hip. There was no time to call James, no time to call anyone. Not when doing so would necessitate her dropping her guard. No way was she going to do that.

She walked around the apiary, which was still shrouded in smoke. She made sure she could see around the sharp corners. She felt a familiar ache in her eyes as her contact lenses picked up the tiny smoky particles from the air. *Don't blink.* Her entire body clenched in response to her futile attempt. She had to find out where he had gone.

There was a sound from where she'd left Patrick. Maybe a moan?

Her eyes started to feel as though they were being shrunk and the lenses were shriveling. Against her will, almost like a seizure, her eyes squeezed shut.

The air shifted around her in that brief moment, and she felt a kind of *swoosh.* Elizabeth ducked, crouching so low that her butt scraped the dirt. She opened her eyes to see a long, metal knife make a sweeping arc that almost skimmed her hair.

Elizabeth rolled to the left and lifted her gun. She shot and missed; he was moving fast. He made another reaching slash with his weapon—a long knife. It hit her outstretched hand, dislodging the gun. Clutching at the deep cut in her palm, she dropped low. She scrambled in the dirt to retrieve her gun. Just before her fingers closed on the handle, he kicked it toward the smoky apiary.

He was on her. A heavy body pushed her into the ground, knees pressing down on her ribs as though he wanted to snap them. His elbow dug into the space between her ribs.

Her arm was already becoming numb. She was pinned.

"Do you know why the smoke stops the bees from attacking?" he asked. She couldn't make out his face through the beekeeper's mask.

She shook her head slightly.

"They are gorging themselves with honey as a last ditch effort to save the hive." He plucked a bee from the ground beside her head and held it in front of her face. As it buzzed furiously, he squeezed the life out of it then dropped its still-vibrating body on her exposed neck. "Pity."

She flinched, but with her arms trapped, she couldn't swat the dying bee away. "Max? Was it you all along?"

"Shut up." His weight suddenly seemed to push down on her even more. He leaned close to her, smelling of cinders and citrus. His hand, sticky and coarse, encircled her neck. "You're nothing like her," he said.

She wanted to ask who "she" was, but her attempt to speak was cut short by his tight grip. She took a short, wheezy breath as her legs started to twitch reflexively beneath him.

"You could *never* replace her."

Elizabeth gasped for air through the limited space

she still had before he cut her off completely. With immense effort, she managed to wheeze, "Easy...to die. Just sleep."

A spark came into his dark eyes. "No, it's not easy. You will suffer."

He abruptly released his grip on her neck and leaned over her face, reaching toward his knife.

The change in position was the opening she'd been looking for. She head-butted him in the chin, hitting him in a way similar to a sharp uppercut. Then she wriggled her leg out from under him and thrust it upward into his groin in a forceful jab.

He only winced for a moment before rallying. It was all Elizabeth needed. She hurled her body forward, hitting the ground next to her gun so hard it knocked the wind out of her body. Her fingers closed around the hilt and she rolled onto her back and pointed the gun skyward.

At nothing.

She leapt onto her feet, each breath coming out shaky and desperate. The hives beside her had become clearer during their struggle, and the bees were venturing into the clearing. The smoke had lifted and they were regrouping.

She gave the stacks a wide arc as she circled them, ears tuned in to anything that might sound like a foot-step. The orange trees rustled gently in the twilight like cowering witnesses.

There was buzzing very close to her ear and she swatted at it absentmindedly. She preferred the bees to their keeper, and found herself backing toward the hives. With a one-handed grip on her gun, she finally pulled her phone out of her pocket and was about to dial when she saw Patrick where she'd left him. He was on the ground

She ran to him, skidding on the dirt and ending up on her knees beside him.

Patrick was clutching his arm and panting heavily. "I think I'm having a heart attack," he gasped.

Elizabeth called for an ambulance, along with backup, then picked up his right hand. "They'll be here soon, okay? You're going to be all right."

CHAPTER 14

Nick dodged a bee, jumping to the side in a harried, frenetic motion. "What the hell happened?"

Elizabeth was sitting on the ground, a good distance away from the hives. They'd already taken Patrick away on a stretcher, having to make the walk to the road both ways with all of their equipment. Nick, James, and any patrol officer in the general vicinity had shown up, too, and were now searching the area. It was a waste of time. He was long gone.

"It was Max Hamish, you know," she said, staring over at the marks in the dirt where he'd tried to hold her down.

"He's the one who attacked you?"

She took a deep tired breath. "He was wearing a beekeeper's suit."

"So you couldn't *positively* ID him."

"No, but he spoke to me and I recognized his voice."

"That's good enough for me. And it makes sense,

considering." The sun was a red ball behind him, like the center of a blood orange.

"Considering what?"

"Linda is missing. There are signs of a struggle next to her car in the Roosevelt Hotel parking lot. Someone took her last night, but when Linda's son's babysitter reported that she hadn't come home, it didn't go through the right channels and we didn't find out about it until an hour ago."

She stood up, dusting off the seat of her pants. "We have to find him before he hurts her."

Nick frowned and looked at her softly, head tilted to one side. "He might have already done it. He was here with you today, after all."

"Dr. Kamen said that the killer kept Alice alive for a couple of days. There is hope, Nick. I won't give up."

"Hey, I'm not giving up, either." He walked away, phone to his ear, barking out orders. He wasn't going to waste the time it would take for them to personally go to Max's house. SWAT could be mobilized immediately.

James came over. "Are you okay?"

"I'm fine. It was just a little scuffle."

Shaking his head, he grabbed her by the wrist and lifted her arm. His gaze traveled across her skin and he repeated the motion on her other arm. He stopped at her hand, holding it open in his palm. "You have defensive wounds."

She followed his gaze and focused on the red gash intersecting her palm. "It's nothing. Just itches a little bit."

"You might need stitches."

She closed her hand and stepped back. "All I want is Linda, safe at home."

"You heard Nick. He's getting SWAT on Max. Let's

get you fixed up while we wait to hear the news." He looked up at the sky. "We need to go to the station anyway for official instructions for the hurricane and its aftermath. Only four or five more hours now."

"Maybe there's something more—"

"No, we're leaving. Now." He pushed her along, impervious to her digging her heels into the ground.

~

THE NEXT FOUR hours passed in the blink of an eye.

Elizabeth had her hand stitched up and properly wrapped while she glared at Nick. She begged him to think of something else they could do. It wasn't long before news came back from the SWAT team they'd sent to Max's place. He wasn't there, and there was no sign that anything had ever happened in that house. He must have taken Linda somewhere else.

After Elizabeth got out of the ER, they personally checked every place that had been significant to the case so far. Each was empty. Max—and Linda, for that matter—was nowhere to be found.

James deposited a coffee cup on the desk in front of him. As she watched, he balled up a napkin and pushed it to the bottom of the cup. He did that to conceal his tobacco spit.

Elizabeth stared at the television mounted high on the wall behind him. It was muted, but she was accustomed to evaluating weather reports by sight alone. It was a huge storm, almost as wide as the entire state. It had a distinctive eye with sharp edges. The large eye would be passing over the center of Miami, which meant they'd experience the worst of the winds when they passed through the two eye walls. Inside the station, Elizabeth could hear the rain pounding on the roof, never letting her forget that no matter how dry it was indoors, conditions outside were declining fast.

Drawing circles on her small desk with the tip of her finger, she said, “So that's it, then, right? We'll have to resume our search tomorrow.”

James tapped his foot in a rapid staccato. “Unfortunately. Especially since we don't have the slightest clue where he's holing up.”

She blinked back tears. “I feel so helpless. And I feel personally responsible for Linda being taken. I can't even think about her being dead.”

“It isn’t your fault.”

“I also shot and killed a suspect. He wasn’t even guilty.”

“According to Max, George killed his mother.”

“According to a serial killer,” she replied scornfully.

James spit a wad into his cup then leaned back in the chair with a loud creak. “My daughter is also having a really hard time with everything. My long hours, the lack of personal attention."

It took her a moment to change gears. "I'm sure Miami is a lot different from Bradenton."

"You have no idea." He slid the cup across the surface of the desk, the waxed paper making a plaintive squeak. "The kids seem to be so much older mentally. She came home from school the other day asking what a French kiss was."

"Maybe you could put her in a different school. Pinecrest is a drive, but I hear it's a lot better."

"She was better off in Bradenton. A lot of things were better." The cup continued to hold his full attention, as did the drumbeat he was banging out with the toe of his boot.

"I'm sorry."

His chin seemed to drop closer to his chest and he spoke in a low, gravelly tone. "Never mind. I shouldn't even be bringing it up, considering what we're up against. You're right about Linda. We should have had an officer keeping an eye on her."

"I know. And now her son might be without a mother. He's only three years old."

Nick signaled her from his desk, gesturing for her to come over.

James rolled his eyes. "What's going on with you and Nick, anyway?"

"Nothing more than the usual harassment."

"Uh-huh." He waved her away. "Go talk to him. He looks like he's going to pee his pants."

Elizabeth wanted to say more, but she figured too much protestation would make him even more suspicious. So she walked away calmly and went to Nick's desk. She glared down at him. "Try to be a little more subtle."

"What?" he asked with an innocent expression. "I just wanted to touch base with you about tonight. I thought I could come home with you. We can ride out the storm together. I was thinking I could pick up some fun stuff to make a special night of it."

"I'm sure the Pleasure Emporium is already closed."

"No, they're open twenty-four hours." He grinned. "That's not the kind of 'fun stuff' I was talking about, you pervert. I meant ice cream, a few good movies, maybe a game. Sex isn't *all* I think about."

"I meant what I said last night."

"That I'm the best lover you've ever had?"

Elizabeth covered her eyes with her hand, weakly

shaking her head. Then she looked up and saw James watching them with interest from across the room.

James quickly looked away when he realized he'd been caught.

"People are already starting to suspect that something is up, including James. It's just like I told you. The gossip is going to kill me."

"Why do you care what they think?"

"I don't know. Maybe I am using gossip as a convenient excuse."

He leaned closer. "Maybe you are."

"All I know is that dating a coworker hasn't worked out well for me in the past. I don't want to make a habit of it. I'd rather be alone tonight."

He shook his head. "Don't forget that the person who put honey in your bed must have been Max. He's still out there."

"To get to me, he'd have to go through a category four hurricane. I'll take my chances."

"Don't be stubborn, Stratton."

She would have punched him in the chest if it wouldn't have been noticed by everyone within watching distance. "Get over yourself, Nick. I'm going home *alone*."

ELIZABETH SAT cross-legged on the couch, trying to distract herself by watching an old Cary Grant movie on cable. All of the networks were consumed with hurricane coverage, but there were only so many times she could watch rookie reporters almost get blown away like old lawn chairs. And she knew what was going on with the storm. It was happening just outside her rattling windows. It was in its beginning stages: mostly wind with a weird kind of rain that sounded like someone was throwing handfuls of water at her windows in no apparent pattern.

She hadn't even considered evacuating. The absolute worst-case scenario would have to befall her before she'd be in any real danger. Granted, her overconfidence was probably a product of having lived in Florida too long. Hurricanes sucked, but after a while she'd started to worry more about possible property damage than physical danger. As long as she wasn't outside in the thick of things, she had no worries.

Besides, if she was going to wallow in her own misery, she preferred to do it in the comfort of her home.

She couldn't shake the feeling that she should have been able to figure this case out. With nervous energy, she bounded from the couch and retrieved the case file from the floor of the hallway where she'd dropped it earlier in a fit of disgust. She spread everything out on her dining table and stepped back to take it all in.

Words on reports blurred before her eyes and a sharp pain started behind her right ear. She closed her eyes tightly for a moment and then resumed her study. She picked up a few photos and examined them, hoping something new would jump out at her. Then she sat down and reread her notes on everyone she'd interviewed along the way. It was useless. Nothing formed itself out of the clay. It needed more guidance from her tired hands.

The ringing in her ears told her it was time to stop, but she didn't want to give up. She rested her head in her hands and stared down at the tabletop.

The pictures from the two crime scenes were laid

out side by side. From the abandoned house and backyard apiary, she assumed she was using Dave's photos. She hated to give him credit for anything, but the quality was beautiful. And if she had to look at depressing pictures, they might as well be nicely composed. The hotel pictures, on the other hand, were stark and harsh.

Even so, they seemed to match. She supposed that made sense. After all, Dave had explored both locations.

She sat up straighter, her heart beating in sync with the gusts of wind rising and falling outside. Dave—stupid, clueless Dave—had done her a favor by bleeding within the confines of her crime scene. How else would she have known that the Roosevelt Hotel was a place urban explorers had crept about? If only she'd realized the importance of that sooner.

She got out her list of the phone numbers of everyone even remotely attached to the case and dialed Dave's number.

Her heart sang when she heard him pick up.

"Hello, Dave? This is Detective Stratton." She couldn't keep the excitement out of her voice, even though she realized he'd probably think she was high or something.

He didn't seem to notice. "What did I do now?"

"You didn't do anything. I'm calling for information."

"Really? Like what?"

She walked around the room nervously. Toulouse thought it was a game and tried to trip her by curling around her legs. "When we asked you about going to the Roosevelt Hotel, you said that you'd heard there was a bee infestation."

"That's right."

She took a deep breath. "How did you know that? Who told you?"

He made a nervous sound. "Are you sure you aren't trying to trip me up?"

"Positive. Please, Dave, answer the question. This is *very* important."

"Okay," he said, "it was on the urban explorer forum where I'm a member. Somebody posted about it, said it wasn't a good option for exploring."

"And the abandoned house where you found the body." Her heart was beating as quickly as it did after an hour on the treadmill. "Were you warned away from there, too? I could have sworn one of your friends said something like that."

"Yes, I was. I didn't listen, but yeah. They said it was very dangerous and that the city had condemned it."

She froze in the middle of her kitchen, tightly gripping the edge of the cold granite countertop. "This is very important, Dave: was it the same person?"

There were a few ums and ahs, before he replied, "I'm not sure."

"Do you still have power? Can you check the forum? PLEASE!"

He put her on hold and went to check.

Elizabeth tried to take some calming breaths. She was so close.

Finally Dave came back on the line. "You're right. It was the same guy."

"That's just perfect," she said, hurrying back into the living room and nearly falling over Toulouse again. The cat squawked and ran off into the bedroom. "Did the guy warn you away from any other places?"

"Let's see..." The sound of tapping keys echoed over

the phone line. "Yes, an old house and barn in unincorporated Miami-Dade."

"Address?"

He had to look it up in his personal records, but in a few moments, he was reading it to her over the phone.

"Thank you, Dave. I'm sorry about all the harassment. You've been really helpful."

"Helpful enough to deserve a call to the Detroit PD asking for leniency?"

"We'll see," she said, but she figured she'd do it. Assuming, of course, she could get him to promise to cool it with the trespassing. "Gotta run."

Her view from the sliding glass door indicated that the winds were kicking up to their worst level yet. The old King Palm in her backyard looked like it was going to bend in two, its top branches caressing the ground.

She shoved the phone into her jeans pocket, reached up into the top shelf of her bedroom closet, and pulled out her seldom-used shoulder holster. She grabbed a dark, hooded windbreaker to go on top.

The driving sound of the hurricane sounded like a high speed train was about to run into her house. It was getting louder by the moment, which meant that the city would be in the eye soon. The perfect time to move. She still had time to spare, so she dialed James, pacing relentlessly in front of the coffee table.

"How are you holding up?" he asked.

"I think I figured it out," she said without preamble. "Where Max is holding her."

"How? Where?"

She explained her reasoning to him and told him about the call to Dave. "I think he's an urban explorer. Or at least, he trolls the urban explorer websites. He planted the bees at the hotel to keep people away so his crime would remain hidden. Then with the house, he said it was going to be condemned."

James made a sound of surprise. "And the pictures! He must have come across them so quickly because he was already been familiar with Dave's blog. I always thought it was strange that the killer would immediately discover the pictures."

"So the place where Linda is could only be the other location he warned the urban explorers away from. Or at least, it's our best shot."

"Which is where?" James asked.

"An abandoned farmhouse out in Coral Gables." She put him on speaker while she texted him the address.

"Okay. I've got the television on channel four and a backup radio in case I lose electricity. The minute the winds get down to a safe level, I'll meet you at your house. Better if we agree to it now, in case the cellular circuits get overloaded. Which they will if the power goes out."

Elizabeth sighed. "This is a slow moving storm."

"And?"

"The winds aren't going to be safe for another few hours. I've had the TV on, too."

"Well, I wish that weren't the case, but there's nothing we can do. Maybe Max isn't even with her right now. He might be hunkering down somewhere a hell of a lot safer than an old farmstead."

She changed the channel and turned up the volume on the television. Outside, the rain had died down along with the wind, and an eerie quiet had taken its place. The reporter on the flickering screen in front of her confirmed her suspicion. They'd just entered the eye of the storm.

"I wish we could have figured this out before the damn hurricane hit," he said.

Elizabeth moved quickly. She herded Toulouse into the bathroom, just in case a window blew out, and left her with sufficient food and water. "You and me both, but at least we know now."

"As soon as this thing is over, we move. I'll call Nick."

She double-checked the bullets in her gun and put an extra clip in her jacket pocket along with a pair of handcuffs. "I'm going after him now."

"Are you crazy?"

"It's the eye of the storm. I should have at least an hour to grab him—"

"Don't even think about it! Everybody knows you don't go outside during the eye. It may look nice and calm, but it can start back up with no warning. You don't want to get caught in that."

"Like I said, the storm is moving slowly, and it's a large eye."

"Forget it, Elizabeth. Besides the hurricane, this is a violent guy we're talking about. You've seen what he did to those women. He won't hesitate to do the same to you." He paused, then continued, "He already *tried* to do it to you."

She unlocked her car with a handheld remote and opened the door.

"Please do not tell me that the sound I just heard was you getting into your car."

"I'm sorry, James. If I find out tomorrow that he killed Linda today, I won't be able to live with myself for giving him the chance to do it."

"Listen, Elizabeth." He seemed to be trying to pull the words together. "You're trying to prove yourself after everything that's happened. I get it, but this isn't the way."

She swallowed over a lump in her throat. "That may be part of it, but that's not the whole thing. I *know* Linda. She isn't some faceless stranger. That makes it different."

"Look, I'll meet you there. I'll see if Nick will come, too. Take your time getting there so we can catch up."

Even though he couldn't see her, she found herself shaking her head. "I don't know how long the eye will last. There's no time to waste. And anyway, what about your daughter?"

"Eh, she wanted to hang out with the neighbor's kids anyway. She'll probably think me leaving was the best thing that could have happened."

She started up her car and pulled out into the empty street. "What about the danger, James? You have a child, and I can't let you—"

"Stop it right there. You're going to have to get used to me being by your side, regardless of the risk. Sure, it might be better for my family if I were an English professor, but I'm not. This is what I do. I'm not about to start doing it half-assed."

"Fine. I'll look out for you, but I'm not going to wait."

"Just be careful."

Elizabeth sped down the empty street, avoiding traffic lights that had fallen into the road and palm fronds that were the size of her car. It looked like a post-apocalyptic landscape. She gripped the steering wheel tightly and drove on.

CHAPTER 15

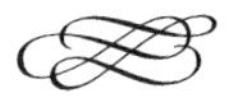

The abandoned house was bordering a murky canal, just over a small bridge. The eye of the storm was holding for the time being, and the air was still heavy with the awful lack of motion that made birds quiet and cows run in circles.

She decided to back up and park just behind the bridge so that he wouldn't have any warning. Then she made the quiet walk to the house, trying to be aware of what was going on from every direction. Wiping damp palms on her pants, she started to crouch when she was closer to the house, using trees and bushes to shield herself. Then she listened.

She heard nothing. No obvious moans of distress; just unsettling silence. She crept closer to the house, heart pounding madly. She unholstered her gun and held it at her side. Stretching her arm out as far as she could, she rapped on the door and hung to the side. She was away from both of the windows and the door. If he opened the door and curiously peeked outside, she would be ready for him.

Catching herself holding her breath, she exhaled in a nervous, stuttering way, determined that not even her barely audible bodily functions would announce her presence. She took another quick look at her surroundings and waited. Then, suddenly, after she had just about decided that it was a lost cause, she heard a sound from inside the house.

She froze, waiting for the slightest squeak. She squatted, but aimed her weapon at chest level. Her hands were shaking as she switched the safety off on her gun, her thumb working almost of its own volition. She remembered exactly what Max had done to Karina, Alice, and Rachel. She'd lain awake many nights, unable to stop seeing their bruised and beaten bodies. Elizabeth didn't want to be the next person on the morgue table while Dr. Kamen made off-color quips. *I'm sure Elizabeth would have shaved her legs if she'd known that today was the day she'd die.*

Max yanked open the door abruptly and took a stumbling step onto the porch. He was just as she'd seen him last: in beekeeper's garb from head to toe, with a heavy veil covering his face.

She almost fell back onto the concrete porch, her finger touching the trigger ever so slightly. *Calm down, calm down, calm down.* She was breathing heavily. She had to do this right. She would not shoot him. Elizabeth forced herself to speak, choosing her words carefully. "Max Hamish, you're under arrest for the murder of Karina Brookes, Alice English, and Rachel Johnson. If you'll just come with me, it will be easier for everyone. I don't want you to get hurt."

He nodded rapidly, the white hood bouncing up and down.

Good. No need to be a quick draw. Elizabeth stood

up, her gun still trained on him. She was about to reach into the pocket holding the handcuffs when the hair on the back of her neck stood up. She glanced behind her quickly and, when she saw nothing, she turned back to the hooded figure, who was now jerking uncomfortably toward her. "You're not Max, are you?"

The person quickly turned to one side, revealing both arms tied behind their back.

Elizabeth strode forward, yanked off the veil, and looked into Linda's dark eyes. There was a wide strip of duct tape covering her mouth. A thick, golden liquid was dripping from breaks in the tape, and she was struggling to breathe through her nose. "Oh, no."

At that moment, Linda's eyes grew big and she seemed to gesture with her head in panicked motions. Elizabeth dodged to the right, toward the wall of the house, just in time to see a long block of wood swinging through the air in the place she'd just vacated. She whirled, moving her gun in a wide arc toward her attacker.

Max was quick. The minute his weapon didn't hit, he ran past her to reclaim his victim. One of his arms snaked around the Linda's neck, then he produced a long, sharp knife with the other.

Elizabeth cocked her weapon. Looking into Max Hamish's eyes, she saw none of the sad confusion she'd witnessed at George's house. It was all vindictive hatred now, and she was scared. "Drop the weapon, Max."

"You interrupted us at a crucial moment. I'm not finished with her."

"Yes, you are." She positioned the gun so that it was pointed at his head and made a conscious effort not to reveal the doubts crowding her mind. She'd never take that shot. Her aim just wasn't that reliable. The question was: did he know it?

In response, Max carefully positioned the knife so that he could slice through Linda's throat in one quick motion. He pulled her toward the open air and away from the sad little house, dragging her with his leg hooked around her ankle. "You came alone."

"Did I?"

He laughed. "Happened to catch the news lately? We're in the middle of a hurricane."

Elizabeth listened closely to the sounds all around her, wondering how long the eye would hold. "Is that why you took this opportunity to take another victim?"

He shrugged. "I just couldn't help myself. I've wanted Linda for years."

Elizabeth moved to get a better shot.

It almost seemed as though he were ignoring her. He was now on the grass, moving toward the canal that snaked its way through the middle of the community.

"If you let her go and come with me now—"

"Save it," he said, dragging Linda a few more feet. "I've already won myself the death penalty. There's nothing you can offer me in exchange for cooperating. Don't come any closer."

Testing him, she moved her leg ever so slightly in his direction.

With brutal precision, he pierced Linda's skin with the tip of his knife and she jerked violently in his arms. With the tape covering her mouth, her screams only produced a haunting guttural sound.

Elizabeth waited. Her entire body shook, telling her to shoot. He was going to kill her, so she might as well take him out at the same time. If he killed Linda in front of her, he'd lose his hostage and then it would be hunting season for her. With this exact thought coursing through her brain, she said, "You can't kill her, because then it's all over."

"Why did you come out in the middle of a storm to save someone you barely even know?"

"Why is it so important to you that you kill her?"

"A bitch just like her stole my father from my mother. She seemed like a waste of DNA to me, but I guess she was good enough for him. That bitch ruined my life. Trust me, I'm doing the world a favor by getting rid of people like her." He looked up at the sky. "We don't have time for this."

The wind was starting to pick up, whistling through the willows lining the canal. A dose of rain sprayed her face like sharp pins. "You're mad at the wrong person, Max. Stop blaming that woman—whoever she was—for sleeping with your father. Your father made his choice, and he was the one who had to live with it."

"No, I was the one who had to live with it! And my mother died for it!" A gust of wind swept through the yard at that moment and he hurled Linda with all his might into the still waters of the canal.

Elizabeth had been jarred by the gust, her feet losing their firm purchase on the grass. It was the advantage Max had been looking for. She got off one quick shot at his rapidly retreating form, but it sailed harmlessly through the humid air. And then there wasn't any more time to think or give chase. She ran toward the water. Linda didn't have a chance on her own with her arms bound and her mouth gagged.

The cloying bathwater warmth of the canal was more of a shock than freezing water would have been. Linda's head had just gone beneath the water. Elizabeth focused on the spot she'd seen her go under. She dove, feeling restrained by her bulky clothing, and swept her arms in front of her in large motions. She didn't feel anything touch her fingertips but slimy refuse and something sharp that made her instinctively yank back her hand. Then she thrust forward again, feeling sick inside.

Her arm brushed against something solid that was jerking like a fish on a hook. It was Linda. Elizabeth hugged Linda's body and pushed toward the surface only a couple of feet away. They broke the surface and she opened her eyes. Linda was fighting her, pupils rolling into the back of her head.

Elizabeth dug her fingers into a tiny spot of tape that been penetrated by the honey and water. She ripped it off in one violent motion. Linda recoiled in shock and pain, small red welts marring the skin around her mouth. Elizabeth dragged her through the water with hard, stubborn strokes, ignoring the panicked convulsions.

She'd only swam for a few seconds before a shadow crossed the bank. Elizabeth fell back as she looked for the source. The sight of James standing there in full attack gear was invigorating. He helped her out of the water and laid Linda on the grass, patting her on the cheeks a few times. "Hey, are you okay?"

Linda hiccupped and let out a low wail. She was nodding and sobbing at the same time as James gave her a quick once-over. "Where is Max?" he asked Elizabeth as he unbound Linda's wrists, keeping his eye on anything and everything.

"He made a run for it. I couldn't chase him and save Linda."

"He couldn't have gone far."

"I saw a large barn a quarter of a mile behind the house. That's the only place he could have run to."

There was a squeal of tires behind them. A moment later Nick ran up to them, simultaneously scanning the horizon for unseen dangers. "What's the latest?"

Elizabeth took a few steps away, shaking the water out of her gun. "Linda needs to go to the hospital."

"All right," he said without argument. "I'll take her."

The end of Elizabeth's weapon exploded in a sharp burst as she shot a stray bullet into the canal. "Good. It still works. Let's get him. We can make up time by driving across the field."

ELIZABETH RAN TO THE CAR, barely giving James a chance to catch up.

Suddenly, James was there beside her, opening the driver's side door. "I think you're free to shoot this one," he said.

"I'm not making any promises one way or the other," she said.

They both hopped in the car. James fell silent, focusing on the drive, going off the road and right into the field. She felt a little tingle in the pit of her stomach. Was that pride? Then the bumpy ride nearly made her head hit the top of the car, and she remembered where she was. It wasn't over yet.

"He's going to have the advantage," she said. "He'll know the layout of the barn and can hide wherever he wants, and we'll be clueless, especially in the dark. And he knows we want to get away before the storm picks up. We have a deadline."

"Then we'll have to change things to our advantage."

James sped up when he saw the barn, his goal in sight. He parked close and they got out of the car. Max knew they were coming for him. This was no stealth mission. As she got out of the car, Elizabeth felt the calm before the storm wash over her. Nothing was moving, not even the slightest breeze. It was as if the earth was standing still, waiting.

Elizabeth was ready. She walked the last few yards to the barn and pushed open the front door with her left arm, not knowing what to expect inside. In her right hand, she extended her gun into the dark interior. No sound greeted their entry. Except for one that was horribly familiar. Bees.

It was yet another apiary, and this one was a doozy. The large barn was full of bee boxes.

Even without the bees, the barn wasn't a good structure to wait out a hurricane. Every piece of wood holding the place up seemed to be rife with wormholes and termite damage. Thankfully the place wasn't too big, which would make a systematic search for Max easier. Of course, Max was now wearing a full bee suit, while the two of them were in nothing more protective than jeans.

The light was dim; mostly moonlight coming in through the cracks in the walls and ceiling. She could hear the bees everywhere, buzzing in harmony. It was like nothing she'd ever heard before, like the difference between one cricket and a thousand. James touched his flashlight, which was hanging from his hip. "Could he possibly have a gun?"

That had been her concern, as well. In the light available, they'd be sitting ducks. "I don't think that's his style." She felt a bee land on her arm with a light tickling sensation. She brushed it off with a reflexive jerk and it took flight.

They scanned the front part of the barn, looking behind a couple piles of scrap wood and a small junk heap, but it quickly became apparent that Max had moved toward the back. Elizabeth took a chance and stepped into the empty area in front of the hive boxes, calling out to Max, "You're not just going to hide, are you?"

James grinned and added his voice to hers. "We're not going away, buddy. What's your game plan?"

Suddenly there was a high pitched keening from the back of the barn—one long, one short—and it was silent again.

"What the hell was that?" Elizabeth shivered and did a full three-sixty degree turn, looking around her. There were too many hidden alcoves, too many places where a man could hide. But that sound had not come from a man.

"Sounded like some kind of machinery."

The long, whiny sound started up again, lasted for a few seconds, then cut off. The sound echoed strangely in the barn. The bees' buzzing was making a drone-like white noise that filled Elizabeth's head and make her want to close her eyes and huddle in the corner. Or lock herself in a padded room.

She felt a sharp pinch on the back of her arm. At the same time, James was turning in circles and swatting at bees. Then she saw that she, too, was surrounded. The buzzing was hypnotizing her, and then, above it all, the high-pitched wail began, and this time it didn't stop. She found herself backing toward the sliver of light coming through the cracked-open door.

James grabbed her arm and dragged her out into the

moonlight. As soon as she was out of the barn, she heard a different kind of sound. Wind.

James was still smacking various parts of his body. "It's like he told them to attack!"

Elizabeth scratched her arm and saw three different welts forming on her skin. "We're running out of time, James! We have to go back in."

He seemed to take a deep breath. "What happened to coming up with a better plan? You can die from bee stings, especially so many. Those bees think we're invading their home."

"Maybe we can go through a back door. He was clearly up to something back there."

"That sound we heard—I think it might have been a saw. That would mean he's armed."

She shook her head. "Guns work from a distance. Saws don't."

"You were more involved in this whole bee thing during the investigation. Did you learn anything about them? Like what calms them?"

"Smoke," she said, immediately. "They fill a small can with fuel, tinder, and petroleum, light it, and fill the hive with the smoke. The bees retreat into the hive and start preparing themselves in case they need to abandon ship."

"Maybe we can light a torch. I can get in there quickly, grab some of that scrap wood that's lying around, and run back out. I've got to have a lighter in my trunk."

"Your crap might finally come in handy." She sighed. "A torch, though? I don't know if fire bothers them. It's a reasonable assumption…but I think it's more about the smoke. So this torch is going to have to smolder. Maybe if we blow on it? Like an incense stick?"

"We've got to try something. This eye can't last forever, and backup is out of the question."

Elizabeth ran to the car and popped open the trunk. She rooted around, looking for a lighter, a remnant from James's smoking days. She tossed aside a baseball glove, two gas masks, and an old yearbook. Then she froze and looked at the two gas masks. She picked them up and ran back to James. She held them out. "How well do these things work?"

"They should help prevent us from breathing in the smoke. I'll grab the wood."

She looked at their surroundings. The field wasn't dry grass and the house was a distance away. She couldn't see any other homes or structures. The canal snaked past the field about a mile to the east, and to the west was emptiness. She remembered the news reports she'd had on when she was still at home. This was a wet hurricane with a massive amount of rainfall. "I have an even better idea. Put on the gas mask."

"What are you going to do?"

She struck up the lighter. "I'm going to set the whole building on fire."

"What?"

"He'll be forced to leave his little fort, and we'll have the upper hand. If he tries to make a run for it, we shoot."

"And what about the fire?"

"Best case scenario: the hurricane puts it out. We're dead center in the path of a category four. This is going to be just like when Andrew hit Homestead. This barn will never make it through the rest of the storm, anyway. It's more important to me that Max doesn't get the chance to kill another woman."

"Fine, let's do it. We're running out of time." He held

out his hand for the lighter. She tossed it to him and ran after him back into the barn. The change in the barn was immediately apparent. There were more bees than ever, and Elizabeth could finally see why. The hive boxes were torn apart, sawed into by Max in an attempt to release the insects. The honeycomb-covered frames were lying everywhere. An empty roof panel illuminated Max from behind in his white beekeeper's suit, giving him an eerie halo. And he already had a ring of smoke around him from a small smoker.

James—now looking like a SWAT team member, complete with gas mask—made quick work of the scrap heap, moving it into place and setting the lighter to it.

Max was shaking his head. "What are you doing?" he yelled.

"Smoking you out." Elizabeth took a torch from James and touched it to an old wooden frame. It caught immediately, a thick plume of smoke rising toward the ceiling.

Max took a step forward, the long silver knife he'd threatened Linda with glinting in his hand. "Stop it! You'll kill all of them."

"You've left us no choice," Elizabeth said. She held her gun out in front of her and was still as a statue, hoping that if she stood completely still, the bees would ignore her to some extent. She was stung a few more times, even as the smoke increased. "I prefer it to the alternative of more women dying at your hands. And you seem to have already sacrificed the bees with your little trick."

He guffawed. "That doesn't hurt them. They don't need that structure to survive. Bees are content to make their home anywhere."

The fire was growing. She would need her mask soon, and she wouldn't be able to talk to Max through it. "Give yourself up, Max. There are only two ways this can end. Why don't you choose jail?"

"Remember when I told you my father killed my mother with honey? The apiary was mine. I didn't know that the flowers he planted would ruin it, but *he* did, and he let me give her the honey every single day. I was slowly killing her."

"When did you find out?"

"Three weeks ago. He wasn't even ashamed."

Elizabeth lowered her mask over her mouth. The smoke was building up rapidly. Already the bees were starting to leave her alone. She held out her gun and approached the back of the barn. Max was coughing violently and she could no longer see him.

She took another few careful steps, then saw James approach. He was hugging the wall of the barn.

Smoke was everywhere, hovering in the air and creating an impenetrable fog. Elizabeth was glad of the mask stifling her ability to talk. She had some kind of psychological need to try to resolve things with words.

Then she felt a whoosh of air next to her and knew words wouldn't cut it. She ducked and felt something sail over her head. Looking up, she saw Max.

He coughed violently and backed away, but he was still carrying the large knife.

Elizabeth wasn't about to put down her guard. She pointed her gun at Max's chest, center of mass. "It's over, Max. Drop the knife."

"Go ahead. Shoot me."

"I want to. I really do." Her finger itched on the trigger. Max was a horrible human being and the world wouldn't miss him.

He hunched over, coughing violently. “Do it!”

Her eyes narrowed on him through her gun's sight. She focused on where the bullet would hit and visualized it going through his chest. “No,” she said, more to herself than anything. “I'm better than that.”

James appeared out of the smoke and jumped Max from behind. Max vomited into the dirt floor as James put handcuffs on him. Elizabeth barely resisted the urge to clap as James dragged Max out of the barn.

When they got him outside, Max collapsed onto the ground and James let him. Max rolled onto his back and stared up at the moon pitifully.

It was nearly imperceptible, but Elizabeth sensed that the weather had changed again. The hurricane was moving. "We need to get out of here," she said, realizing that they were still in danger.

James looked back at the farmhouse a half-mile away. "Do you think?"

She shuddered, thinking of what Linda must have endured. She was still wondering how she'd stayed alive. She supposed Max enjoyed playing with her. "I'll take my chances with the drive. But I don't want to make any decisions for you—"

"We're in this together. I'll never let you ride alone. By now, you should know that.”

Max had stopped coughing and was now sneering up at her. “Those bitches deserved everything they got, especially the first one.”

“And why is that?” she asked.

“She went with my dad, just like the others used to after my mother died. All a bunch of whores, easy for him to get into bed. And I had to wait around while he did it.” He laughed. “Ironic, isn't it? He didn't want to leave me home alone, but he thought it was okay to take me with him on his *dates*."

James yanked Max to his feet and pushed him toward the car.

"Sometimes he made me watch. Every one of his sluts looked like the complete opposite of my mother; it was like he couldn't bear to have someone who looked like her," Max continued, even as James pushed him into the back seat.

They didn't have an official police car with a protective cage, so James retrieved another pair of handcuffs and shackled Max's legs on the tightest setting just to be safe.

"The toy car. Was that you?"

He laughed without humor. "That craphole was one of the places he took dates while I played on the floor."

Elizabeth turned around in her seat, unable to resist more questions. "So you followed George out of the hotel bar and waited until he walked away from Karina?"

"No," he said, smiling. "I got them both to come with me to the empty floor. Told them it would be fun to explore. Then, when we got to the last suite, it was my turn. I made *him* watch while I banged his whore. He left after a little bit."

"And you?"

"I guess I got carried away. You should have seen it, what I did to her. She—"

"This conversation is over," James replied and turned up the stereo.

They managed to make it back to the station before the winds escalated. They threw Max into a temporary cell, and then they were stuck at headquarters until the storm passed. Elizabeth and James played poker in the break room, drinking way too much coffee and raiding the captain's desk for junk food until the hurricane broke at dawn.

ELIZABETH TURNED to leave the hospital room where Patrick was recuperating and in doing so almost knocked the two cups of coffee James was carrying right onto his chest. She chastised him playfully. "Don't sneak up on a girl like that."

"Just testing out my ninja skills. I guess I need to work on them some more." He looked past her toward Patrick's room. "I knew I'd find you here. I thought we were meeting downstairs in five? It's been a lot more than five."

She shook her head and accepted the cup of coffee he handed her. "I'm sorry. I was on my way. I just wanted to make sure he was okay. I feel awful for asking him to come with me that day."

"You couldn't have known what was going to happen. It was just a bunch of bees."

"I don't think I'll ever think of them as *just bees* ever again."

James nodded to a cute woman at the nurses' station they passed. "What about Linda? How's she doing?"

Elizabeth felt like her heart was beating in her throat. "She's traumatized. There's no denying it, but she's a strong woman. I think she'll get through this."

"I'd like to see her sometime, but I don't know if she'd like that."

"Are you kidding me? Linda considers you a hero." Elizabeth hooked her arm through his as they walked.

"So what do you think now that our first case is over? We made pretty good partners, right?"

James nodded and walked onto the elevator. "You wouldn't go back to Chris? I heard you two made quite the team."

"What else have you heard?"

"Nothing." He stared up at the elevator panel as it counted down the floors.

Elizabeth sighed and pretended she believed him. "I prefer you to Chris, but it doesn't matter. He transferred and he isn't coming back."

"Actually he *is* coming back. Apparently, Captain McQuinn supports his return one hundred percent."

She had a sinking feeling in the pit of her stomach. "That will be interesting."

"You're telling me."

"But I'm not going to let it ruin my day. Here," she said, handing him a tin of chewing tobacco. "I thought you deserved a little something for braving the eye of the storm with me. We're lucky we didn't end up in Oz."

"Thanks, Elizabeth," he said with a grateful nod. "Would you like some?"

She shook her head with a smile. "Although that tobacco is the finest on the market according to the clerk at the 7-Eleven, I'm still going to have to pass."

Moments later, they sat in the Crown Victoria, listening to the tinny scanner. The report of a double murder came through. "We're on it," James reported back.

With unrestrained glee, James turned on the lights. They were on I-95, on a long stretch of lonely, empty highway, and he gunned it. The sound of tires on wet asphalt and a purring engine filled the interior of the car, and Elizabeth let the white noise put her into a trance.

She looked down at the city of Miami splayed out before her in thousands of sparkling lights. When she squinted her eyes, the lights blurred at the edges until they resembled little starbursts. And even though she knew what lurked beneath the haze, she couldn't help but think it beautiful.